What it is to Bleed

Maddy Rose

Book Cover by Panagiotos Lampridis, 52Design Studio

First Paperback Edition June 2025

ISBN 979-8-9985297-0-2 (paperback)

For a younger me, who didn't think she could do anything.

Chapter 1

I was never one to believe myself worthy of good things. I was never taught that I deserved more than what I earned. Never thought of myself as strong and brave in a world not designed to be strong and brave for me. As a result, I became greasy and nasty, unhealthy and riddled with self-loathing like anything would. At several points in my life, I found I wouldn't be surprised if I woke up the next day dead from alcohol poisoning. The worst part was, I didn't really even care that that possibility was more likely than me living to an old age.

For a long time, I accepted all of that as an inevitability. It became my expectation that I would never deserve or receive anything beyond the bare minimum. I wasn't impassioned enough to think that I'd ever earn more than minimum wage, live somewhere I felt truly at home, or even overcome my addiction. When you spend so much of your life assuming that is all that is destined for you, it becomes your reality.

It nearly did become mine.

I'll never forget the first time I met him. It was like a dream. A dream that sucks the breath from you, waking you up in a cold, burning sweat. I felt that way almost every time I looked at him. Like I could simply melt away and die, so utterly content and rageful with love. I'd never felt that way about someone before. I was a heartless creature. But, just one grumble from the pit of his tender chest sliced me open, splitting me all the way through to my soul.

He saw the light in me that I didn't see in myself.

It was so late. The kind of late where you wonder why you're even still out and panic whenever you see someone else, in the end knowing you're both just judging the other for not being home. The kind of late where everything is quiet to the degree of horrifying, but also in a way that's peaceful compared to the noise of the day. The kind of late that people weren't meant to see. Maybe I was lucky to be awake *and alone* so deeply into the night. At least, I thought I was.

I was working my second shift, hoping no one was interested in buying anything from this particular Shell off of I-84.

During this last shift, I kept myself facing the front of the store at all times. I just had a bad feeling about being here so late again. The previous few nights this week, a man kept coming in at about the same time, buying a pack of gum and only that without ever saying a word. He never did anything threatening. Buying gum isn't indicative of a crime, but it just kept me on edge. I wasn't sure if I was being scouted or stalked or softened for when a real attack came. I feared his goal was to make me complacent. I was determined not to become so.

At half past 3, I decided to move myself from behind the counter and occupy my hands, almost willing my anticipation to disappear. If I didn't, I probably would've picked all the skin off my arms or worse opened a bottle of beer. It wouldn't have been the first time. Although, ever since I got caught wasted on the clock, I've been much more vigilant and perhaps secretive about my habits. Truthfully, I was more afraid of my manager than the gum guy. My job had more value to me than my life anyway. So if anything, my lack of complacency was from fear of being laid off.

I distractedly grabbed the ugly yellow mop bucket on wheels, pushing it out into one of the aisles. My arms felt like quaking weights, shaking with both anxiety and ginger sobriety. All the same, I dunked the mop into the bubbly mess, then started to spread it out across the tiles. Methodically, I leaned back and forth with the movement, almost dancing to my work. It was lulling in a way, pinching my mind with the reminder of tiredness.

Maybe that's why I always compared our first meeting with a dream. Perhaps it was one. I was half asleep anyway, leaning against the mop pole, wanting to be high on something other than bleach.

It wasn't long before I couldn't take it anymore. Leaving the mop in the aisle, I half-jogged back to the register, pulling out a hidden 50ml Fireball. I humored myself by calling it my "emergency medicine", but I used it too much and had to restock too many times a week for that to be true. The lid chaffed my fingertips a little as I twisted the cap open, downing the entire thing in one go.

I'd become so used to this routine, I knew how long it would take to hit. I just had to stall until then. It wouldn't get me completely fucked up. It would just stave off the restlessness, so I could actually do my job. Just get through the night really.

I found the mop again and got to work. The more my "medicine" kicked in, the slower my cleaning was, but the cleaning was only busywork. If I made it a few more hours puttering around like this, I could go home, and another day would be done. I could mark it off on my calendar with the kind label "survived".

Unexpectedly, the sound of a car pulling up to the front of the station startled me. I was so used to this sound, and instinctively, I began mopping more violently as if whomever was about to walk in would expect me to. From where I ended up from my cleaning, I could only see the top of the door over the tops of the shelves. I waited, braced myself almost, for the sound of the bell dinging to alert me of a customer, and, just like I predicted, it happened. It felt so loud in that moment, stinging my ears with the reverb.

I heard gentle footsteps begin to walk around and the sound of keys bouncing in a pocket. It seemed to be only one person with very distinctly soft footsteps very much unlike the gum guy's. Realizing this, I was able to settle my heart palpitations just a bit, which had come on so suddenly.

Putting the mop I'd had a death hold on back into the bucket, I shuffled myself around the shelves to the front of the store. I could see the back of the customer, who crouched low, looking at something from in front of the counter. I could tell at once that this was not who I was afraid of.

"Can I help you find something?" I asked, making my way to the register.

Hearing my voice, he stood up quickly, throwing his hood off his head, revealing a gorgeous thatch of dark, brown curls. His equally dark eyes dove straight through me, and I felt almost naked in front of him. His gaze was soft, however, so I didn't feel uncomfortable.

"Um, I was just looking. Could I get a pack of Marlboro, though?"

His voice was unique and intriguing. Deep and thick.

I noticed as he moved, he wore delicate gold chains around his neck and had a few small tattoos on his face and throat.

"Anything else?" I asked, reaching behind me, grabbing what he'd asked for, then setting it on the counter and pushing it towards him.

"Nope, thanks."

I watched as his long fingers fumbled through his wallet for a ten, handing it to me when he'd snagged it. He smiled at me with slightly yellowed teeth, scrunching his nose up with genuinity. I punched the keys on the register like I had a hundred times, handing a receipt to the stranger when I was done. The interaction was informal, but long, in my head, at least. For a second, it didn't feel like this was a stranger at all.

As he took the receipt from my hand, another customer pushed open the door, ringing the bell. My eyes darted to the door, honestly expecting to see the customer before me reenter, rendering these past few minutes an illusion. But, instead, standing in the doorway was a middle-aged man in a bright red hoodie, long shorts, and beat up Jordan's. I recognized him immediately. He shoved his hands deep in his pockets as I watched him slowly walk towards the counter. The customer I was checking out took a step closer to me, placing his hand beside mine. Both of us were staring at the man, who cleared his throat loudly and said:

"Open the register."

I blinked stupidly. It was the gum guy.

"I said open the register." he repeated.

The customer at the counter turned to me, shaking his head.

"Don't look at her! Look at me!"

The man at the door drew something from his pocket and it took me a minute to realize what it was. The gun he held was small, mostly black with gray accents around the handle. He held it shakily in his right hand, his eyes raging with adrenaline.

"What do you think you're doing?" The words with a tone of defiance left my mouth before I understood what I was doing. I wasn't courageous. I suppose the Fireball just hit quicker than I expected.

"Bitch, what the fuck did you just say to me?"

"Get out of here. I'm not giving you anything."

I glared back as the obvious shock that was spread across the man's face morphed into a merciless fury. In the same moment his shaking hand stilled, he pointed the gun to the glass case behind me, squeezing the trigger with little force. The bullet flew past me, bursting through the drug case, sending shards of sharp glass all over my back. I could feel bits falling into my shirt while others sliced into my neck, splattering small droplets of blood onto the register. The customer ducked down out of the way, covering his face with one of his hands.

"Open the goddamn register, cunt!" the man repeated.

I ducked as he fired another bullet in my direction. I could hear it whistling as it soared by my ear, missing me by mere inches. I screamed, throwing myself out from behind the counter. The customer was laying on the floor just on the other side. He reached out a hand to grab me as I scooted myself closer to him, pulling me swiftly away from the glass that littered the floor.

The gunman shouted with rage, stomping towards us. The customer kicked his legs out, stopping the man for a second as the bottom of his shoes collided with his shins. I scrambled up to my feet in that brief moment, running into the closest aisle. I heard the muffled sound of more kicking, but I couldn't quite tell who was getting hit.

"Fuck you!" the man bellowed, shooting another shot.

His arm must've been pinned or pointed upwards because the shot flew directly into one of the ceiling lights, shattering it into millions of pieces. Other than a loud grunting, there was silence from the other side of the aisle, then, suddenly, the customer darted around the corner, flying towards me. Just behind him, the man with the gun followed, chasing with some difficulty given his weight.

Without thinking, I threw my arms up to the shelves, shoving down boxes of cereal onto the floor. The customer saw what I was doing, jumping over them before he could trip, but the gunman wasn't as quick. His large left foot landed on a box of Cheerios, acting as an ice skate as he slid forward, his heavy body flying in my direction.

I went to back away, but I wasn't fast enough. The man reached out his hands and grabbed my shirt, bringing me down to the ground with him. My head and torso hit the tile aggressively, knocking the breath out of me for a few seconds. In the time that I spent gasping, the man straddled me, drawing his hands up to my neck. He wrapped both his meaty hands around it, applying unrelenting force to my throat, leaning his whole body into me.

I tried pushing him off, but he was too strong. It was like pushing against a brick wall. No matter how hard I tried, he wouldn't budge. Gradually, the room around me started to fade as I floated from consciousness. All I could see was the man's vulgar face, his mouth spitting rotten saliva, his eyes bloodshot, pupils enlarged. I couldn't believe that was the last thing I would ever see.

"STOP!" I heard someone shout although my hearing had grown faint.

Like it was thrown from a slingshot, a can of soup suddenly flew over my head, hitting the man that choked me square in the chest. It shocked him just as much as it shocked me, and he let go momentarily. As he released my neck, I drew my knees up to my chest, pushing him away from me with a brutal kick to his gut. He yelled out, flailing his arms upward as a result of his unbalance.

Powerful hands scooped me up by my armpits, dragging me backwards towards the refrigerators on the opposite side of the room. I looked up to find that same stranger from before. I had honestly thought he'd run, but it seemed he hadn't. It then occurred to me too that he had been the one to throw the soup can.

Reality set in as I steadied myself, my face beginning to gush with furious tears. We only had seconds before the man would be back on his feet. I wasted no time moving back towards the front of the store, heading straight for the door. The stranger followed me, but so did the gunman. As I placed my hand on the handle of the door, the glass on it burst from the impact of another bullet.

Both of us whipped around to face him. He was seething with anger, his chest rising and falling with large intense breaths.

"I'll shoot you this time, I fucking swear it." he gasped, walking towards us, one slow step at a time.

The fear that choked me gave me only one option. Quiet sobs echoed in my chest as I moved like I was being remote controlled back towards the counter. I held my shaking hands up the entire time, not taking my eyes off the guy for even a second. He watched me tiptoe behind the register, and then as I took the key out from under the secret place on the bottom of the counter. I unlocked the drawer with a click. As he heard it, the gunman jogged towards me, his gun still pointed at my face.

Sensing what he had to do, the customer leapt forward in a flash, thrusting himself at the man with a grunt of force. He tackled him to the ground, shoving the gun out of the way. The robber shot another few shots as they wrestled, both wheezing for breath. The customer, this complete stranger locked on to the man with a determination like no other, kicking his arms, trying to get the gun away.

As I watched like nothing more than a spectator, I saw an opportunity. For a fleeting second, I almost ran away. But, something inside me begged me to be brave. And so I was.

With hands moving quickly on their own, I reached down below the counter again and grabbed a short knife I had stashed in the far corner. I gripped it intensely in my palm as I proceeded to throw myself over the counter, propelling my way into the fight. Tossing the customer out of the way so that he flew into one of the shelves, I bent over the man and slit his wrist that was holding the gun. He fired reactively, then it dropped at his side. He yelped out in pain, but I couldn't hear anything other than the vicious beating of my heart against my eardrums. I laid myself on top of the man's legs, keeping him as still as I could, sinking the knife into his gut. I could hear him choking on blood, but I only watched as his eyes rolled back into his head, the faint whispers of breath leaving him faster than I anticipated.

When his head finally relaxed and hit the cold tile, I sat back onto my heels, looking at what I'd done.

The customer was panting tired breaths beside me, staring at the side of my face like he could've burned a hole through it. The legs of my pants had begun to soak up the hot, sticky substance oozing from the wound. The feeling of it reaching my own skin froze me where I sat, forcing me to realize what had happened.

"What did we do?" the customer mumbled, pushing himself up off the ground.

With no thoughts in my mind, I reached over, grabbing the gun and throwing it away from the massive pool of filth that was beginning to develop. The knife was still sticking out of the man's lower abdomen, blocking a good portion of blood from spilling out everywhere. I debated for a moment whether I should leave it there, but decided quickly I should take it. Closing my eyes, I bent over, gliding it out like I was playing Operation. I could feel the squelching of flesh as I maneuvered out the blade, cringing at the sound of it.

I didn't turn back to look at his body once I'd removed my weapon, wiping it across my chest to remove the vile burning liquid that soaked it. I could feel tears welling up in my eyes once more, but fought them back so as not to embarrass myself yet again in front of this savior of a stranger.

For a second, both the customer and I stood looking at each other. The gentleness of the stranger's eyes made the tightness in my chest ease a little, but I couldn't help but feel an aching sense of self-loathing at what I'd just done.

The stranger seemed as if he were about to say something, but just as he was going to speak, I heard the sound of another car pulling up to the station. I knew what this looked like. And I knew what I had done.

"I can't stay here," I whispered, breathing violently. I stared into the eyes of the customer, without thinking about what I was about to say. "Do you want to come with me?"

This wondrous stranger had no words himself, but, from what I could tell was a very deep and broken place within him, he nodded.

Without hesitation, I leapt across the room to the counter where I'd stashed my keys and backpack. I took both, swinging the backpack over my shoulder, then scrambling out towards the back of the store. With much more elegance than myself, the stranger followed, running up behind me and staying within a foot's distance.

I led us into the blackness of the storage room where there was an alternate exit to the parking lot. Towers of boxes surrounded us, deadening the sound of our shoes squeaking with wet blood against the tile. The cover of darkness benefited us, giving us extra time I knew we didn't have.

Once we got to the backdoor, I pressed my body up against it savagely, sending it open into the windy evening. I made sure the customer got out before I closed it behind us, and we darted for my car that was parked just next to the dumpster.

"Get in, get in, get in!"

After throwing my bag into the back seat, I jumped into the driver's side, twisting the key, now smeared with blood too, to start the engine, and immediately reversed around the station. I switched off my lights, made sure I didn't see anyone looking in the parking lot, then sped off onto the highway, not bothering to peer back in my mirror as we disappeared.

Chapter 2

The night was raging. The sun had long since set, the only lights for miles being the occasional neon sign alerting to another gas station or motel. I laid heavily on the gas, flooring it down the endless stretch of concrete. I kept my eyes glued straight forward, but I could tell my unexpected guest was staring me down from beside me. I bit my lip hard to keep from crying as my conscience slowly started setting in. In the moment, I'd been reckless and angry, but now I would give anything to go back and change it all.

I already hated who I was and what my life was. This was the worst possible thing that could've happened to me.

"Um, are you okay?" I mumbled, glancing around nervously.

"Yeah. You?"

I sucked my tongue in, feeling my chest tighten. "Mhm."

My eyes darted back and forth along the road ahead of us, searching for something I wasn't sure of. In my frenzy, I saw my bloodied hands, every crease on my fingers filled deep with sticky wetness. We needed to clean up. It wouldn't be long before the man was found. Before we were found.

Up ahead, I saw a 24 hour laundromat next to a McDonald's just off the exit. Mechanically, I turned us off the highway, up the ramp to the bridge above us and crossed it. Across the street from where we were headed, in the parking lot of a 24 hour liquor store, a group of dark clothed men sat together around motorcycles, seemingly smoking a joint. They were the only people anywhere around us, so I noted their presence.

"Look," I started, pulling into the parking lot of the laundry. "I have no idea who you are, and I can take you somewhere if you need to be somewhere, but I can't take you back. You didn't do anything wrong. You're innocent-"

"So are you?"

I stared blankly at him. "I'm not. I just ki..kil-" I couldn't say it.

"He had you at gunpoint. You were scared! What do you mean?"

I couldn't admit it to this beautiful stranger now, but I wasn't innocent at all. At least, not in the eyes of the law. The problem was: I wasn't sober. If the police found me now, I'd be most definitely convicted for murder.

I felt so utterly trapped.

"Listen," the tears came again and my voice started to shake. "There were cameras all over the station. They know I was working. They can look at the footage and see us both."

"But, why did you run? If they see all that, they'll know it was self-defense."

"Why did you follow?"

He looked at me, a hopeless longing in his eyes. "I don't know why. I wanted to make sure you're safe."

"And that makes you an accomplice."

The reality sunk in for both of us. Regardless of what we did or didn't do ten minutes ago, we'd chosen to run. That in itself was a crime.

"Alright then. What do we do?" he asked.

"I need to get out of these clothes. The smell is gonna make me vomit. Look at yourself, too." I gestured to his chest, which was drenched in blood and glass.

"Okay. In here, right?"

I nodded, opening my car door.

The moment I stepped out, I could hear the men behind us, laughing amongst themselves, loudly and obnoxiously. I only took a peek at them from the corner of my eye, noticing a few of them were looking our way. Keeping my head down, I turned towards the laundromat, walking up a few stairs at the entrance, then heading inside.

The fluorescents were blinding, but, oddly, the sound of a dozen washing machines tumbling was calming. I could see a woman working behind the counter on the other side of the store, wearing headphones and reading a magazine. She didn't acknowledge us at all; only bobbed her head to her music, keeping very much to herself.

From where we stood, I could see the bathrooms off to the right of the store and motioned for the stranger to head that way.

"Take off your clothes and come back out in your underwear. We'll try to wash them at the front of the store, so she can't see us."

He understood, heading into the mens as I walked through the swinging door to the womens. The lights inside were off by default, so I switched them on, unknowingly starting up a heavy fan in the ceiling. The vibrations that reverberated around the room made me feel sudden nausea. Maybe it was the intoxication, maybe the adrenaline, or maybe the disgusting realization that was slowly starting to envelop me that I had in fact just stabbed a man to death with one clean thrust.

I hobbled over to the sink, feeling the urge to be sick. I gripped the edges of the porcelain roughly, leaning over, coughing and retching.

The vile, burning, acidic projectile practically exploded from me the second my head fell forward, spilling out through both my mouth and nose. Involuntary tears streamed down my face as my cheeks began to get hot and achy. I gasped audibly, coughing up leftover mucus.

"Fuckkk."

My distress was clearly not blocked by the stupid fan above me because in only a few seconds, the bathroom door swung open, revealing the stranger, standing there in nothing but boxers. You couldn't tell before, but he was absolutely jacked. Not in necessarily a traditional sense of slim and muscular, but he was thick and full with strength. His abs, although soft, glimmered with sweat, and his shoulders, heaving with each breath, tensed and relaxed over and over with an odd sense of physicality. The chains I'd noticed him wear earlier laid so tenderly on his collarbones, shiny and glistening with the same sweat. And, probably his most striking feature were the dainty tattoos covering his arms and chest. I hadn't seen the extent of them before under his sweatshirt.

He rushed over to me, scooping my hair out from behind my wet neck, holding it up out of the way.

I could hear him laugh. "You were totally wasted, weren't you?"

"No!" I sniffled. "Maybe a little."

"So, that's why you're so defiant. You do have something to be guilty of."

I stood up straight, leering into the handsome stranger's eyes.

He only smiled. "I figured as much."

I shook my head, raising my hand to my mouth to wipe it. I'd almost forgotten it was blood covered and nearly smeared the dried remnants all over myself.

"Here." the stranger offered, grabbing a few paper towels and handing them to me.

"Why are you not mad? Why not turn me in now?" I asked, so utterly confused at the amusement in his eyes.

"I'm not exactly in the best position to do that. I mean...for starters, I'm Latino."

I couldn't help but laugh. Even though what we were talking about was horrid, I couldn't help but feel a sense of relief in this stranger's presence. The feeling was strangely enough...safety.

"Plus, I have a bad feeling about this. I don't know what's going to happen, but I think we should stick together just until we find out what to do. C'mere."

My stomach tightened at his words, but I let myself fall towards him as he took my hands in his. Pulling me over to the sink, he turned on the faucet, guiding my hands under the warm water. With gentility, he massaged crappy soap in between my fingers, washing away every nasty inch of them. When my hands were clean, he grabbed the base of my shirt, beginning to pull it up over my head. He looked at me for permission and I nodded, holding my arms up above me. Easily, he pulled it off, tossing it to the side after. I undid the button on my jeans, sliding them down myself, handing them back to the stranger once I'd pulled them out from under my feet.

My mouth was bitterly dry, tasting of everything I'd just expelled from it. As a remedy, I bent my head low under the faucet, slurping up a few gulps of the gross tasting water. Except, the water wasn't gross at all. To my acid coated throat, it was like an ice bath, washing away every fiber of pain. Once I'd completely satisfied myself, I wiped my mouth with the back of my now clean hand, standing up to look at myself in the mirror. Mascara dripped from underneath my bloodshot eyes in a black pool on my cheeks, and all across my face, splattered there like freckles was blood. The longer I stared, the harder it was to breathe, watching the monster I didn't recognize in the mirror.

"I'll take these out. You stay here if you want?" the stranger offered, snapping me away and indicating my clothes.

I shook my head. "Could I come with you?"

"Yeah, sure."

I followed him out closely, crossing my hands in front of me to cover my chest. I felt so awkward shuffling around in my socks, panties, and bra, but not awkward in the sense that I felt embarrassed. It was weird. It was almost awkward in the sense that it was normal.

"Oh, fuck. I didn't bring in any money." I realized.

"Nah, it's okay. I brought in my wallet." the stranger revealed, showing me the same wallet he'd used earlier to pay for cigarettes.

I watched him as he put in a few quarters and shoved our bloodied clothes into a washing machine at the front of the store. The woman in the back was still distractedly humming to her music, either unaware of us or too underpaid to care. Where we had situated ourselves was one row of washing machines behind the large glass windows at the front, so no one from the outside could see in, but we could still see out. From where we stood, I could still spot the men across the street. Since I'd seen them last, there were a few missing, but the ones that remained had moved their bikes closer to the street.

"So, um, I'm Nicky." the stranger mumbled, turning towards me and leaning against the washer.

"Kasi." I nodded back to him, rubbing my face with my hands.

"I like that."

I smiled. "Thanks."

"So, what'd you'd take?"

I was caught off guard by the question. "What?"

"To get so high?"

"Oh, I just drank a little."

"A little?"

I rolled my eyes. "I don't usually."

"Ah, I see." I could see him smirk at me from the side as he sat down on the floor.

I sat with him, leaning against the machines and letting the vibrations numb my back. It was a nice, uncomfortable feeling. Just enough to make me forget about the painful pressing of tears against my eyes.

"Here, want one?" he suddenly asked, pulling a cigarette out of his wallet.

I took it, placing it between my lips with shaking fingers. He drew a lighter out of the wallet too, lowering it towards my face. I could feel his eyes on me as he lit the end of my cig, such softness in his every movement. Once it caught, I inhaled quickly, taking a huge drag and letting the smoke waft around me. Nicky took one out after me, lighting it as well.

We didn't speak the whole time we waited, both of us almost motionless except for the occasional drawing of our cigs. In many ways, it felt like we were sitting there forever, but it also ended too soon. The precious moments of security we had on that dumb fucking tile floor, freezing our bare asses off, was taken entirely too fast. The tears I'd been fighting nearly broke through my crusted lashes the second I heard the dryer finish our clothes some forty-five-ish minutes later.

I would be lying if I said I didn't thoroughly enjoy the feeling of warm clothes against my back again, but putting on clothes that had been (and still partially were) blood stained made my skin crawl. I saw so many precise images flash across the backs of my eyelids of the knife in my hand and the moment I witnessed the life fade from the eyes of the robber. And then the look, oh that fucking look, on Nicky's face when I saw him next.

The reminder of what I'd done to this stranger made me incredibly insecure, riddled with guilt and self-consciousness. I could imagine the endless resentment I was about to be faced with in addition to the incoming and unrelenting sense of terror as the consequences of my actions were brought to me.

Despite all the moral turmoil I felt, there was only one thing on my mind. I longed so desperately for the burn of any kind of alcohol down my throat. Even after all the vomiting I'd just experienced. Any time I ever let myself feel things this strongly, I was always quick to wash them away. It had been a long time since I'd been so vulnerable with myself.

I wasn't ready to face it.

"Um, do you have any more money?" I asked, full well knowing I had no right to ask this near complete stranger for anything.

Nicky looked at me, confusion on his face, but he didn't say a thing. I watched as he put his sweatshirt back on over his bare chest and belted his loose jeans back up. Once he had knotted up his bandana belt at the front of his waist, he handed me a twenty dollar bill, trading it for the cigarette I'd been holding.

I took it quickly like it was on fire, stuffing it under one of my bra straps, then bent over to put on my bloodied white Converse from the pile of clothes we'd been unable to wash. With my jacket over my shoulder, I bowed once to Nicky and left out the front of the store, walking straight past the car towards the street.

Before crossing, I turned around, looking for Nicky, and saw him standing beside the car, watching me. One of his hands was in his pocket, the other holding his cigarette to his lips. He seemed to study me as if I were some odd puzzle he had yet to solve. Granted, I was some odd puzzle I'd had yet to solve, so I didn't blame him. I just felt so absolutely undressed by him. Every usually unnoticed decision or action I took was now being watched by this stranger.

A couple of the bikers from earlier were still in the parking lot across from me, laughing and talking. I made sure to cross as far down the street from them as I could, walking all the way across the back of the parking lot to avoid any interaction with them. Of course, they noticed me instantly, whistling and such, but no one made any advancements.

Men like that always scared me, but for the first time in my life, I felt genuine horror at the thought of them. And at the thoughts I had surrounding the horror I felt. It surprised me how easily I could imagine pulling the trigger on their heart or slamming a baseball bat into the back of their head. I could practically feel a knife in my hand, slitting their throats slowly and viciously. Violence, rage, and fear hadn't always gone hand in hand for me, but I wasn't sure anymore.

Much like the door in the Shell, the door of the liquor store opened with a bell, alerting the cashier of my presence. I saw a tall and lanky older man raise his eyes to mine behind the register, his mouth grinding back and forth from tobacco in his mouth.

"Howdy." he nodded his head firmly to me.

"Hi."

I knew exactly where I was going. Even wasted as fuck, I knew how to navigate a liquor store better than my own apartment. Immediately, I went straight for the back, grabbing a bottle of vodka, a bottle of wine, and a six pack of Coors. The vodka was slim enough I could slide in one of the interior pockets of my leather letterman. That's why it was my favorite. I had to be careful though. The way the man at the counter was watching me gave me such a sense of looming anxiety. He couldn't have seen me hide the vodka in my jacket, but he almost seemed to know me.

"That all for today?" he asked as I set the wine and Coors on the counter.

"Yep."

"Can I see an ID?"

I remembered I'd left my wallet in my backpack in the car. I hadn't thought of this before coming over. Well, I hadn't really been thinking much at all recently.

"At home, sorry." I muttered, putting one of my hands on the counter to steady myself. The fear had turned into dizziness and vertigo just as quickly as it had turned into nausea. I noticed my fingers were still bloodstained, the underneath of my nails clogged with chunky blood.

"That'll be fifteen then." he decided, tiredness in his voice.

I handed him the twenty, stuffing my hands in my pockets to keep him from seeing the blood, and also from anxiously wringing them around my already bruised neck. Once he'd rung everything up, he slid them into a plastic bag, handing it to me cautiously.

"You have a good night, love. Be careful out there."

I should've just shook my head and left, but instead, I dumbly asked. "What do you mean by that?"

He hesitated before speaking. "There was a stabbing just a little ways from here. Whoever did it got away. They said it was in a Shell."

"Oh, yeah."

I felt like vomiting again. My head clouded over, and my eyes felt like they were about to beat out of my skull.

"You alright, miss?"

"Yeah, yeah, I'm fine."

If I could've sprinted, I would've, but I probably would have passed out before I got too far. I hated having to walk past the bikers, and all I wanted was just to see Nicky again. I thought maybe just one comforting look from him would settle this panic that had settled on my chest. To be fair to myself though, that wasn't the only thing I wanted. Before I'd even gotten halfway across the parking lot, I pulled the vodka out of my jacket, opened the top and took a large swig. The familiar burn of fermentation coated the inside of my throat, and the pain distracted from the intense nausea. It was a dangerous kind of pain to enjoy, but I couldn't ever get a big enough fix of it.

"Momma, need a ride home?" one of the bikers asked me, watching me stumble over myself as they startled me.

I flipped them off with the same hand I held the vodka with, then continued onto the sidewalk. I didn't look before crossing, but found I wasn't really worried about being hit. I kinda almost wanted to be.

The blinding lights from the laundromat led me up the inclined parking lot like a stairway to heaven, guiding me straight back to the car where I'd assumed Nicky would be. I even lowered myself to the window to look for him, but he was gone. The only sign of him was a cigarette butt on the ground, wafting up a little smoke.

Behind me I heard sudden footsteps running up the concrete. I didn't know him well, but I knew these couldn't have been Nicky's. As they reached me, my heart stopped.

Chapter 3

My gaze fell to the bottle in my hand, and I suddenly became very self conscious. "Nicky?" I called out.

"Need help, darling?" a deep voice grumbled.

I gasped, spinning on my heel to meet one of the bikers from across the street. He was large and oily, smelling strongly of weed and child support. He smiled at me devilishly, leaning in closer and closer. I clumsily backed away, clutching my vodka bottle to my chest.

"No, thanks." I spat with much more confidence than I felt.

The laundromat door swung shut.

"Hey, who are you?"

It was Nicky. He bounced down the stairs, walking right in between us and taking the things from my hands. He opened the car door, shoving them inside, blocking me with his body

The biker backed off a little, observing the situation. He didn't speak for a moment, surprise and confusion on his face.

"Sorry, babe." he whispered, looking at me, backing himself out of the parking lot with his hands up in front of him in surrender.

I could hear his friends laughing at him from across the street, but didn't turn to see.

"Sorry, I just went to the bathroom." Nicky mumbled, staring at me guiltily.

"No, it's fine," I whispered back to him. "You don't owe me anything."

He made a funny noise in his throat like he disagreed with me. "Okay then. We should get out of here."

I nodded to him, beginning to get into the car, but Nicky put his arm out in front of me.

"Could I drive?" he asked.

"Why?"

"I saw what you gulped down just a minute ago."

I laughed to myself to hide the embarrassment, then awkwardly walked around to the other side of the car. He slid in after me, setting the bottles into my lap.

He sensed my heart. "It's okay."

I took what he said seriously, unscrewing the vodka bottle lid and taking another swig. The same adrenaline rush of fiery poison gliding through me soothed any uneasiness I'd had. It completely ruined me. Well, it ruined my brain. I was so infatuated with the taste and the feeling of the heavy bottle in my hand I didn't notice we'd left until five or so minutes later. I only realized when Nicky swerved back onto the highway and the car built up speed.

Usually when I drink enough to get myself off, I start to feel everything around me so vividly. This time was no different. All the colors and sounds were so vibrant like I've never seen them before. My hands felt like they weren't attached to my body and all my limbs felt both light as a feather and heavy as a boulder. I felt as if I was running even though I was sitting. Even driving, it felt like I was in the Flintstones car, moving my feet so quickly below me, sending the car speeding down the long stretch of pavement.

In reality though, it was Nicky guiding the movements I felt. I didn't know him, but I trusted him more than I trusted myself. That was probably a weirder feeling than the out of body high I was experiencing. Sitting next to him, I could imagine myself in a movie, looking hopelessly out the window, watching raindrops race each other down the glass like cars. A sense of freedom encompassed me, alluding to the clear lack of self awareness I'd donned since drinking nearly half a liter of straight alcohol.

It was so easy to do. To be honest, I'd had a lot of practice, but the shifting of myself into a mindless reality had become almost second nature. After half an hour of not knowing where we were going or what our plan was, I seemingly disappeared from the car altogether. So deep in my mind, everything around me was bliss.

I imagined myself leaning against someone, laying in my underwear on a bed. My head was perched so gently in their lap while they played with my hair, using only the very tips of their delicate fingers. Their voice was deep and soothing, almost entrancing me in a sleepy sense of comfort. I let myself relax into them, closing my eyes and nuzzling my nose into their leg.

But, just as I began to inhale a large whiff of their musk, my hands and arms and legs and feet became alarmingly wet. I sat up quickly only to find myself drenched in blood. It dripped down me in fat gobs, bubbling and burning numerous cuts and scrapes along my skin. I tried to wipe it off, but it just kept coming. And coming. And coming.

I yelped out, not in pain, but in fear, unable to find the source of the bleeding. I checked my body all over, trying to feel for a wound, but, still, nothing. With a sense of urgency, I leapt up from the bed, dashing across the room to a standing mirror. When I approached it, however, I found not myself standing there, but Nicky. I was looking straight at him, him looking straight back at me. There was a look of disappointment on his face and I soon discovered why.

Buried deep in his chest was a knife. The same knife I'd used to kill the gum guy.

I watched Nicky's mouth open to scream, but just as the piercing screech began to ring out, a hand took my shoulder, yanking me out of the dream.

"Kasi!" the real Nicky's voice gasped.

My eyes bolted open, frantically darting around.

"I think you were dreaming. You're all sweaty."

I glanced down at myself, feeling the dampness press against my neck. "Sorry."

"Don't apologize. Hey, listen, I've been thinking-"

"Shut up!"

The radio was on a very low volume, but I recognized the sound of breaking news interrupting the rock station. I flung my hand to the knob, twisting it forcefully towards myself to raise the volume.

We interrupt this station now to bring all alert to dangerous persons. 22 year old Kasandra Walt was seen early this morning stabbing a man to death in her workplace: the Shell off of 84. A man was with her who took part in the scuffle; his identity is yet to be discovered, but surveillance footage showed him to be about the same age. Both individuals ran from the establishment after the killing and are currently still avoiding custody. If anyone should happen to see one or both of the individuals, please call ********.

I turned slowly to Nicky whose bottom lip was trembling. "I guess that settles it, then."

"What do you mean?" I asked.

"We can't stay here. We have to get out of here."

26

"But, I don't know you! You're innocent!" I shouted, feeling delayed emotion well up inside me. "Pull over!"

Nicky aggressively swerved the car into the berm, slamming on the brakes.

I jumped out madly, begging to pace. The nausea from earlier returned with a vengeance, clouding my vision. I felt like vomiting again.

"What's going on?" Nicky questioned me, walking out beside me as cars soared by us going 70 plus miles per hour.

"I don't know what to do! I just met you an hour or so ago, and now I got you involved, and I'm gonna go to jail, and I'm gonna lose everything!"

"Listen to me!"

I stopped pacing to stare at him.

"I'm gonna tell you what. I made a choice today to walk into the gas station. I made a choice to tackle the motherfucker who shot a gun at your head. And I made a choice to get into your car and run with you. *I* got myself involved. You're not gonna go to jail because you are going to leave. Leave the state. Get far away from here."

"What about you?"

"What do *you* want me to do?"

I didn't expect that. I honestly didn't know. Some fucked up part of me wanted him to come with me. But, I couldn't ask him that. I couldn't ask a perfect stranger to leave everything they had and do what? Run?

I threw my arms up over my head, trying my best not to slam them into the gravel. I felt as if every part of my body was just attacking me. My heart beat so firmly and boldly, my lungs hesitated in their expansion, tightening in my chest, my head spun, pressing strongly against the back of my eyes, my fingers tremored, my legs ached. I closed my eyes, shielding myself from Nicky's penetrating ogling, covering my face with my hands. I closed my teeth down on my tongue, sucking my cheeks in, doing everything I could to keep from sobbing.

The reality of my situation was becoming clearer and clearer by the second.

Suddenly, I felt two large, warm arms envelop me, drawing me into a soft chest. I could feel Nicky's breaths steadily against his ribcage. I tried to focus my entirety on matching those breaths, sucking air in shakily through my nose and pushing it calmly out my mouth. I don't know how long it took, but the grip he had on me didn't loosen until I'd been able to center myself enough to breathe on my own.

"Come with me." Nicky whispered, releasing me from his embrace.

I didn't take my hands from my face, letting him guide me to what I assumed was the car. He grabbed me by the shoulders and laid me down across the back seat, tucking my bloodied Converse up under me. I took a peep through my fingers to watch him close the door after me, then get in the front once again.

"You know, you are probably one of the bravest people I've ever met." he mumbled, adjusting the mirror so he could see me.

"I'm sorry." I gasped, not able to contain the emotion.

"I'm not." he confidently said, pulling back out onto the freeway.

"You should be."

"Something really bad happened to *both* of us. We got into this mess together. We're gonna get out of this mess together."

Through slits, I followed Nicky's hand as he reached for the radio, turning up the knob once he'd reached it. A popular Amy Winehouse song was playing, and I could feel the reverberations travel throughout the car with hints of her smooth voice.

"Just close your eyes and listen." Nicky encouraged me, adjusting the volume to the goldilocks level.

I did as he said, trying my best to untense my body, melting into the seat.

"Hey, wake up."

Nicky was at my side again, leaning over me through the car door. I scrambled up quickly, anticipating the worst, but only his sweet smile met me. I looked around at where we were and noticed the sunrise. It was warm and gentle, shining meekly over the tops of the buildings and trees that surrounded us. We were in some kind of motel parking lot, judging by the numerous doors lining the beige concrete wall.

"Look, I'm really tired. I think we should sleep here for a few hours. We're almost out of Oregon."

"Okay." I breathed, sliding myself out of the car.

The ground below me felt so still. Or maybe it was me that felt shaky. I couldn't really tell. The mix of anxiety and hangover confused all my senses, only allowing me to feel the bare minimum. Nicky saw my struggle and took my arm under his, leading me to a room on the far end of the bottom strip of doors. I was glad there weren't going to be any stairs involved. I wasn't sure I could muster the strength to climb them.

"We're 201." Nicky mumbled, pulling a key out of his pocket.

It was an old fashioned key; not a keycard like any other hotel would've had. Metal and rusted, it appeared to have seen the hands of hundreds of guests in its day. When Nicky forced it into the lock, the metals made a crunching noise as they rubbed together, grinding against the rust of the other. I cringed at the sound.

In only a moment, Nicky managed to open the door, swinging it inward with a loud screech. I practically fell inside, my eyes darting around to find the bed. Once I found my target, I collapsed down onto it, curling myself up against one of the pillows. The cool cotton pillowcase made my face feel numb, applying such a stark contrast to the feverish heat my whole body girdled.

I heard Nicky close and lock the door behind us, shutting the curtains and placing the chain across the gap. He then strode quickly across the room to the bathroom where he spent only a few minutes. The familiar sound of a toilet flushing and hands being washed prepared me for him to reenter the room, but he didn't. In fact, he stayed in the bathroom for what felt to be another ten minutes, making no sound.

Curiosity took hold of me easily, maneuvering my tired body from the comfort of the bed to the door of the bathroom. I leaned in closely, pressing my ear up to the chilled door, straining myself for something to indicate Nicky's state. What I heard shocked me. Between sharp gasps, I heard the distinct sound of sorrow, undeniable sniffles and tears. I could just picture him on the other side of the door, his back heaving as he tried to muffle his sobs.

The ache of guilt I felt at the sound of his struggle took any remaining strength from my legs, and I sank to the floor, falling into the door. I could tell Nicky was just on the other side, maybe even leaning up against it himself. He didn't seem to have noticed me yet.

"Nicky?" I whispered, pressing my lips up to the surface of wood.

I heard him rapidly scramble to his feet, wrenching open the door as fast as he could. I fell towards him at the speed of the motion, grabbing onto him in the rush. The look on his face as his eyes fell to mine was enough to make a person die inside. He seemed so drained and hopeless. His lips quivered, dripping from the tears streaming down his face.

He made no effort to hide himself from my gaze, kneeling down slowly to match my height. The sight of him brought tears to my own eyes, and I felt as if claws were ripping at me from the inside, bringing a blazing pain to the sinking feeling of helplessness. Without realizing what I was doing, I lifted a hand to his cheek, cupping it in my palm and using my thumb to wipe tears from under his eye.

"We're gonna be okay." I mumbled, trying my best to smile.

In an instant, Nicky had me in a hug, crying intensely over my shoulder. I wrapped my arms back around him almost as quickly as he'd encased mine, clinging onto him so tightly. As he sobbed into me, I sobbed back into his chest. I couldn't help it.

"I'm so sorry." I gasped, tightening and tightening our embrace.

As his breathing slowed, I used what small strength I had to stand us both up, leading us towards the bed. I turned around, so I could back him into it, laying him gently where I had been only a few minutes ago. Just as I had, he curled himself up small, hugging himself into the pillow. I brushed the hair out of his eyes, then drew one of the blankets up over his body, tucking it around him. Afterwards, I removed myself from the bedside, sinking down into the armchair across the room. I watched him, his chest rising and falling as he carefully drifted off to sleep. It didn't take long at all, and before I knew it, a gentle snore escaped his mucus-y nostrils, lulling the room in its quiet darkness.

I noticed as I looked around that Nicky had brought my backpack in with us, setting it across the suitcase stand under the window.

Crawling over with a sensitive step, I took it from its pedestal, wrenching it backwards with me to the chair. I unzipped it mindfully, opening it to find the bottle of wine tucked neatly inside. Without hesitation, I removed it, drawing it close to my chest as I set the backpack back down. Hugging it like a toddler, I unscrewed the lid once I'd peeled off the seal, downing a few gulps as soon as I had.

Like any wine, it was potent and bitter, but it gave a momentary sense of euphoria that made the taste and lip-puckering texture worth it. Almost robotically I sat there, sipping on the liquid straight out of the bottle, watching Nicky like he was part of the scenery. It was so easy to get lost in the methodical motion of drinking that before I knew it, half the bottle was empty and my head once again felt light and airy.

I only noticed how much I'd drank by the sudden lightness of the bottle as I brought it to my lips. It wouldn't have been difficult for me to finish it all, but some stupid ounce of self-restraint, or maybe some guilt perhaps, stopped me. The out of body numbness that was gradually enveloping me made all the raging feelings I'd felt slip away like a toy boat down a river. I could practically feel it being drawn from me as if there was someone with long, dainty fingers plucking away at my body and soul.

It was nice, but I knew I'd regret it.

A car horn hollered outside, sitting me up from my slouched position in the armchair. I launched myself up out of it, darting to the window to take a peek through the blinds. I saw several cars stood waiting at a green light and some small little bug was sitting holding up traffic. In a second or two, they realized their mistake and all the cars carried on as if nothing had happened.

If only it was that easy.

The sound must've woken Nicky slightly because he rolled over onto his back behind me. He spread one of his arms out across the bed, laying the other gingerly across his chest. His face scrunched up with pain, his eyebrows furrowing together, his lips pursing. The longing for a comfort I didn't know drew me to him, and very gently, I climbed up overtop of him to the other side of the bed, sitting straight up against the headboard.

The arm he had stretched out had a few spots of dried blood crusted along its elbow, and subconsciously, I took my thumb and began rubbing away at the remnants. My touch at first startled him, but then his body relaxed, his forehead untensing and his jaw visibly loosening.

I'm not sure what overcame me at that moment, but the urge to cuddle up into the open space beside him became unbearable to resist. Selfishly, I let my longings get the better of me and slowly scooted myself down to creep into his chest. I delicately laid my head against his arm, easing my arms and knees into myself as I leaned into him. Naturally, his arm tightened around me, bringing me in closer and closer to him. I took the opportunity to inhale his affable scent, letting it fill my nose with something other than stiff alcohol.

He was warm and soft and the odd safety I felt at his side made the fight to stay awake breathlessly simple to lose.

Chapter 4

It was probably sometime midafternoon when we both woke up again. Nicky had taken his arm and strewn it across my stomach, clutching me to him. I laid still beside him, my hands thrown over my head into the pillow above me. We were both so lifeless and so silent. Even once we'd both woken, we just laid there, occasionally looking at each other, wanting to say something but not knowing what. Every once in a while, we would hear the sound of someone walking past the room, both our hearts stopping until we knew they hadn't come to knock on the door.

I didn't want to have to break the seal of the sanctuary of rest we'd laid claim to on that bed, but, I really *really* had to piss. My bladder felt like a water balloon about to burst, screaming out for me to relieve it. The slow decrease in adrenaline from the past dozen hours or so had allowed me to feel more and more of myself. I didn't like that. I'd never liked being able to feel myself in my entirety. Not physically or emotionally.

But, damn. I had to fucking piss.

Gently, I moved Nicky's arm back over onto his chest, slipping myself off the edge of the bed and into the bathroom. The floor was sharply cold, sending shock-like spikes of pain up through my calves and into my thighs. I tip-toed hurriedly over to the toilet, squatting down quickly, letting my panties slide down to my ankles. The sweet release of nearly an entire bottle of vodka plus everything else I've drunk since I had dinner yesterday felt like an explosion of warmth.

Burning warmth, though. Not necessarily in the comfortable sense I'd imagined it as I lingered there in bed, trying to convince myself to leave it.

Once I'd finished, I didn't have energy enough to stand, so I simply dropped my elbows to my knees and idled there, sinking my back down lower and lower. While half-conscious, I listened for Nicky and heard the sound of him walking around; doing what, I didn't know.

A sudden knock at the door startled me.

"Yeah?" I shouted, my anxiety cracking my voice.

"It's just me, Kasi. I'm gonna get something to drink out of the vending machine just on the other end of the strip. Want anything? A water, maybe?"

"Okay. Sure, thanks."

"I'll be right back."

The sound of the chain lock on the door being fiddled with and then the distinct sound of the door being swung open met my ears, indicating Nicky's departure. In a similar motion, I found my way to the sink, hanging my limp hands under the frozen water before dousing myself in soap. I hesitated before looking in the mirror, fearful of what hideous thing I was about to see. Much like I anticipated, I looked awful. My face, apart from my flushed cheeks, was pale, vampiric white, blotchy from tears and malnourishment. The usually delicate waves that fell around my face were messy and tangled, the dark brunette stained in places from blood. I took a hand up to it, massaging my scalp, watching my cracked and dry lips shake with near agony.

I felt sobs fill my chest, climbing up my body like viscous monsters, clawing their way into my soul. The easy, tired breaths I'd been taking, quickened with visions and memories, haunting me with the reminder that I had ruined my life.

I rushed out of the bathroom, unable to take it anymore, and threw myself onto the bed, sprawling out as if it could encase me. I remembered the small bit of wine I'd left earlier this morning and instantly flung myself across the room to find it. I couldn't remember where I'd left it...to be frank, some of my memories weren't as clear as others, but I knew I had to have kept it near my other things. Opening my backpack, I threw my hands inside, fumbling around the copious amounts of garbage I usually kept in there. At the sensing of something cool and metallic, I thrust my arm forward, believing I'd found it, but the only thing I felt was excruciating pain.

Unknowingly, I'd grabbed the end of my short knife within my palm like it was the neck of a bottle, crushing my fingers around it with a death-like grip. Because it was nothing less than a weapon (a murder one at that), when I went to yank it towards me, it only sliced me open, splitting my palm like a tender chicken breast.

"FUCK!"

I clutched my hand to my chest, seeing nothing other than oozing blood. In a panic, I'd dropped the knife to the ground, accidentally kicking it across the room. I watched it sitting there now not only covered in the blood of a stranger, but mine as well. It sat there so innocently, knowing full well that it was not at fault for the pain it inflicted. It may have been used to end the life of another, but it had no conscience to remember the way it felt to be shoved into someone's body, piercing organs and flesh.

That was what *I* remembered.

I cried out, rushing back to the bathroom to run my fingers under some water. After clearing some of the blood, I saw how deep the cut was, realizing there was no way I could just put a bandaid on it.

"Fuck! Fuck! Fuck! Fuck!"

Once I rinsed it thoroughly, I took a hand towel off the hanger beside the shower, wrapping it tightly around my palm. The fingers on my left hand were already completely numb, but very soon the aching numbness traveled down my wrist, creeping up towards my elbow.

I needed to find Nicky. I didn't know what to do.

As ungracefully as I'd entered the room, I scurried back out of it, racing to the door with my hand raised in the air, blood dripping down my forearm. With my free hand, I gripped the door knob, preparing to wrench it back towards me. But, suddenly, there was a sound on the other side. A knock, specifically. Loud and booming, entering the room with such an inescapable, terrifying presence. I froze instantly, not knowing what to do.

In a few seconds, they knocked again. Harder this time. It wasn't the typical knuckles to door kind of knock that a housekeeper or a lost neighbor would use. It was a pounding. Fist to wood. I could tell they laid almost their entire forearm parallel to the door as they hammered against it. I knew only a few people that would knock with such horrifying urgency.

"Sheriff Deputy, open up!"

A man. Deep, gruff voice.

My body shaking intensified as I backed away, bringing my hand closer to my chest, whimpering.

The man jiggled the door handle, pounding a few more times.

"Is anyone in there!"

A fleeting feeling of certainty in knowing what to do passed through my clouded mind, dragging me to the closet at the side of the room. The folding doors gave me just enough room to slip behind them, but not before pinching me on my way in. I was careful not to shout at the pain, covering my mouth as I sunk down into the dark corner, pushing the doors closed with my foot. Fearful tears rolled down my cheeks, pooling on my collarbones.

"Nicky, please come back." I whispered, desperately

The small moaning cries escaping my mouth could only be so muffled by my palm, but I just hoped beyond hope that it was enough.

"Hello?" the man hollered, shaking the handle with such force I thought from the sound of it it might just fall right off.

I heard more voices outside, discussing something, then more pounding, then more talking. It continued for what felt like hours even though in reality it most likely only lasted ten minutes. I was in so much pain it was hard to truly discern what was happening around me. Hot blood continued to pour down my arm, dampening my shirt and pants as it had only hours before. I tried wiping it up, but only made more of a mess. Now there was blood on both hands as well as my face from wiping tears.

"Please, Nicky, come back." I sobbed, sniffling snotty sniffles.

At my request, suddenly the voices and the pounding at the door silenced. I could not tell what was happening, but it felt as if they had given up hope of finding someone. Finding me.

Perhaps somewhat stupidly of me, I inched open the closet door with my foot so unbelievably glad to be able to see just a little. The air in the room was fresh and life-giving in great contrast to the stuffiness and bloodied mess of where I was curled up. I sucked in quick breaths, practically gasping for the clean oxygen. Without realizing, I'd been slowly edging my way farther and farther out, exposing myself more and more.

Like a gun firing a bullet, a loud, brutal harassment of the door handle echoed throughout the room, unexpectedly. I tucked myself back into the far corner with mad efficiency, unable to keep my whimpers quiet, for the fear had truly begun to set in. My dirtied hand locked on to my mouth once more, doing what it could to smother my every sound. Even my breathing was becoming suggestive of my location.

To my horror, the door lost its battle in an instant, creaking open, then just as quickly creaking closed. The rush of footsteps pierced my ears, sending a tensing spell all throughout my body. On its own, it was preparing to protect me, even if I myself had no clue how it might manage that in the state I was in.

"Kasi?"

The immediate, sweet relief of a familiar voice.

I practically kicked open the door, falling out onto my knees. Nicky bent down beside me, trying his best to steady me.

"I'm so glad you're back! Someone came to the door, trying to get in. I didn't know what to do." my voice cried out almost totally separate from my head; fast and unnerved.

"Shhh. What happened?" he gasped, noticing my hand.

He took it from me, unwrapping the towel, finding the nastiness below.

"Shit, what'd you do?"

I couldn't look him in the eye. But, the way my selfish body shied away from the knife at the other end of the room couldn't have made it more obvious.

"Kas, did you try to hurt yourself?"

"NO!" I groaned with an accusatory tone. "It was an accident."

I sobbed gently, cowering into the small ball I'd been in seconds ago. Nicky rushed to correct my posture, hoisting me back up onto my feet. He guided me back into the bathroom, lifting me up onto the counter as if I was light. With airy steps and quick footwork, he ran back out into the room, checking the locks on the doors, closing the blinds even tighter than they had been before.

"Kasi, where's your backpack?" he hollered out, rustling around.

"I don't rememb-"

"It's here. I found it."

I jumped a little as he leapt back into the bathroom abruptly, carrying the half empty vodka bottle as well as one of the Coors from yesterday. He opened the Coors with the familiar click and breath of the satisfying freeing of condensed air, then he handed it to me. Pressing the sharp metal edge to my lips, I tipped back the can, letting the tasteless carbonation trickle down my throat.

From where I was sitting, I could see myself in the mirror that hung across from me on the closet door. My face was red, my eyes bloodshot and tired, my mouth and nose covered in blood, my neck streaked and smeared with the same. Sweat collected around my hairline in tiny clustered balls, shimmering against the yellowed, hollywood style light above my head.

"Give me your hand." Nicky asked, wrenching it towards himself rather forcefully.

I kept my eyes focused on my reflection, determined not to feel.

Even though I couldn't see exactly what he was doing, I could picture him as he rinsed my hand first under the one-temperature of water the shabby sink provided, then proceeded to rinse again with the last of my precious stolen vodka.

At least we still had the wine. Well, what little was left of it.

"GAHHH!" I screamed out, my hand burning like a chemical fire.

"I'm sorry." Nicky whispered, a touch of pain in his voice.

I knew he had to do what he did for the purpose of avoiding an infection, and, in many ways, I hated him for how he inflicted more hurt upon me, but I also couldn't keep myself from feeling a strange sense of helpless gratitude. We owed each other nothing, or at minimum, he owed me nothing; and yet, here he was. Helping me. And apologizing

"Stop," I grumbled, drawing his eyes to my own. "Thank you. I mean it."

He nodded solemnly, looking back down to my hand.

With tender fingers, he placed a clean washcloth over my hand, wrapping it around the back. Then, with almost craftsmanlike delicacy he took the thin, bandana belt from his pants and tied it around my palm, squeezing my tissue hard against the washcloth. I winced at the initial searing burn, but after a moment it subsided to only a mild ache.

"What...what happened out there?" I asked, lifting the Coors can to my face once more.

Before I had a chance to even glide my tongue against the edge, Nicky took it from me abruptly, pouring it down the drain, using it to wash away the blood in the sink.

"HEY!" I shoved my good arm against him, forcing him to retreat into the door. "Fuck you."

"Have some water instead. I told you I'd get you one." he said, pulling out a bottle of Dasani from his back pocket.

"To answer your question, I don't really know what happened. I went down to the end of the strip to where that vending machine was, right? But, it wasn't working. The lights all off, you know? So, I had to go inside to the front desk to ask if they had any others. When I went to come back out, I saw them at the door. There had to have been at least 3 or more officers out there. Big burly dudes. Scary as shit."

"What'd you do?"

"Well, the guy at the desk looked freaked and told me to go back to my room. I gave him a look that kinda said 'okay buddy' and he immediately knew. I'm not sure if he felt bad for me or something because he offered to cover for me if I could get out of here in fifteen minutes. Some white savior thing, probably."

"Wait...we have to get out of here?" my tongue shriveled with dread.

"We need to fix this first, though." he breathed, coming close to me again and reaching a hand to my face. He held me steady under his gentle strength while he wet down his other hand and began to wipe away the blood.

His touch absolutely melted me. So tender and yet he moved with urgency and mission. His fingers dragging along my skin from ear to chin, neck to chest. It was almost as if there was no strangeness between us. He treated me as if we'd been friends for a long time, caring for me as if I mattered to him. Both our breathing slowed into faint gasps and whispers, indicating how utterly odd and comfortable this was for each of us.

Once content with his job, Nicky finished with a towel, his eyes engaged so intently on my face. I couldn't help but smile at him, hoping he was too focused to realize. If he did, he didn't show any sign of it, helping me down off the counter, holding me until I'd gained my balance.

"Thank you." I offered again, making sure I locked eyes with him to show my sincerity.

His lips lifted at the edges, hinting at only mild strain. Guilt was the biggest of the feelings I had weighing on me, so it wasn't unexpected when my chest tightened as I examined him. He seemed so young before me even though he couldn't have been any different in age and maturity to me. In many ways, I saw a boy and a man, staring down at me like a wounded deer. Part of me hated that he looked at me like that, but, for once in my life, I didn't feel so hopelessly alone.

"Should we bother to clean up, do you think?" I asked, turning around to find how trashed the bathroom was.

"I don't think we have time. We just need to get our stuff and get out."

"Where will we go?"

Nicky's face dropped. "Not sure. Anywhere?"

It occurred to me that I didn't actually know where we were. I remembered talking about getting out of state, but just wasn't sure how close we were to achieving that goal.

Nicky seemed to read the question on my brows. "We're about two hours from Kennewick. Our best bet might be to make our way over there. We'd be much more hidden in a larger city like that."

I agreed, moving myself away from his observant eye. I tried walking out of the bathroom casually, but I was clumsier than I wanted to admit, tripping over my backpack that'd been left in the doorway.

This was the first time I'd really taken note of my hangover. I drank so much last night (or this morning I guess), it was a miracle I could even stand at all right now. Even still, my lips felt parched. Thirsting for the taste of relief. The promise of relief had been taken so rightly earlier by Nicky, but the pain I felt at failing him once again was not powerful enough to keep me from searching for another can of Coors.

Then I remembered the wine.

Trying to search discreetly, I fiddled my hands around in my backpack, pretending my trip had been somewhat intentional. Nicky brushed past me, his thigh rubbing up against my hip. I felt a small rush of surprise flutter through my body at the feel of him, but it was only fleeting.

As I finally grasped the neck of the bottle, I recalled exactly how much I'd had the night before. Watching Nicky, scrambling to collect our shoes and other things around the room, I unscrewed the top, gasping down the remainder of the bottle.

I found myself quite conscious and insecure about how savagely I indulged in the consumption, but often, I found my *problem* outweighed any feeling of self-hatred. That I had plenty of. But, alcohol. That I had more of.

My eyes stayed glued to Nicky's back as I knelt down, rolling the empty bottle under the bed. I then closed and slung my backpack up over my shoulders, sliding to the door, matching Nicky's urgent pace. While scanning the room, I noticed we left quite a sight in our wake. Blood splatters on the walls and floor, empty, a crumpled beer can, a disheveled, dirtied bed, soiled towels, and a flesh-licked knife...

"Nicky, wait!" I half-shouted, grabbing him as he made an attempt at the door.

"What?"

"The knife. What do we do with it?"

His eyes were confused at first, but then he understood. "Where did you leave it?"

"It's by the closet, I think?" The direction was more of a question than a location.

Nicky crouched low, his eyes flashing back and forth against the dark carpet. In an instant, he found it, but rather than bring it back to me, he wiped it on his clean shirt, then slammed it down into one of the arms of the chair I'd sat in last night.

"They're gonna know we were here anyway. Let's leave them a gift?" he laughed, almost hysterically.

His laugh was contagious, but I could not force myself to smile. "I don't think that's a good idea."

"What do you suggest we do with it instead?"

The sudden change in his tone from caring and concerned to frustrated and confused released a small rage within myself. I couldn't blame him, of course. I'd been so caught up in my own mind. Out of self preservation, maybe. I had almost forgotten he was human, too.

"Just give the fucking thing to me." I sighed, holding out my good hand.

He thrust it out of the cushion, then handed it to me, his face distorted with slightly manic anger. In my heart, I wanted to believe it wasn't me he was truly upset with, but I'd be lying if I said I myself wasn't struggling to find compassion for me.

I clutched the blade to my chest as I turned myself back around, grabbing the door with my fingertips. The movement burned my poorly tended wound, but I was determined to open it without help. The light of the day blinded me when I swung the door backwards. From having the blinds closed, the inside of the motel room had been so dark and misleading as to the condition of the outdoors. Now, I knew how loudly bright it was, the sun beating down with little success at bringing heat.

I could see two police cars, their lights on, parked right up against the curb near the door. No one was inside them, but through the cracked windows, I could hear the radio grumbling out static. I'd been so disoriented when we first got here that I had no clue where to find my car. Nicky was quick to solve that mystery, though, as he rushed his way there as soon as he'd closed and locked the door behind us. I had to skip a little to keep up with him, but the terrifying exhilarance of the moment made it easy.

Nicky didn't even give me a chance to enter the driver's side, hopping in himself with a grunt of effort. We were concealed a bit at the back of the parking lot, but I made sure to keep my eyes on the pavement as I walked to the other side and slid in, still clutching the knife to my chest.

The car began to roll away before I even got the door closed, but I was lucky Nicky had set us in motion, for the sound of more approaching sirens wailed at us from down the long stretch of roadway we were closest to. We pulled out devilishly fast onto the roadway, careening out into traffic. A few cars honked their horns, but Nicky disregarded the attention. Instead, he sped even faster, his foot falling further and further down onto the gas.

The effects of the wine dizzied me as we drove, rocking me with the movement of the car. And maybe it was the impact of the intoxication that led me to do what I did next, but I surely wasn't going to pay it any more thought than that. Because, with a trembling hand, I cranked down my window, throwing the knife out into the grass as hard as I could, watching it fly out away from me never to be seen by anyone ever again.

Chapter 5

"How's your hand?" Nicky asked me about an hour later.

His eyes were straight on the road ahead of us, one fistful of fingers wrapped around the steering wheel, the other laying neatly against the center console. He seemed so stoically strong and content sitting there, which was quite a different picture than what I imagined him looking like on the other side of the bathroom door earlier today. His hair, although disheveled, rested against his eyebrows in gorgeously long locks, almost hiding his exact expressions from view. I found myself wondering if I could've seen beneath the bangs, I would've discovered strain, building up to another outburst of pain.

To be honest, my hand felt horrible. The more I thought about it, the more I realized just how many nerves must've been in my palm, making it feel like I was being branded with hot iron rods over and over again every time I moved. I found holding my wrist with my other hand, practically pinching off the blood supply, gave me a little bit of comfort, but it took all I had to keep my whimpers to myself. When I wasn't watching Nicky at the wheel, I was squeezing my eyes tightly shut while biting my tongue to distract from the agony.

We knew we couldn't stop to pick up any medical supplies or painkillers, at least not until we crossed the state border, so I simply had to hold out until it was safer. Nicky's discernment of my constant reaching for something to drink was becoming more obvious to me, so, for his sake at least, I kept my backpack, which I knew was filled with the Coors, in between my legs. I didn't know exactly why I felt a need to be different for him. Maybe it was the sadness in his eyes, the disapproval on his lips. I don't know. It just filled me with an awful consciousness that felt like pneumonia in my chest.

"I'm alright." I mumbled, massaging my wrist in between my thumb and forefinger.

"You don't sound it."

His eyes met mine, weak with empathy, and I felt a single tear roll down my cheek at the sight of his pain for me.

"Do you uh...have any of those Coors left?" he asked, his gaze falling down in between my thighs.

"I think so."

"Have some."

"But-"

He cut me off by turning up the radio. We'd been sitting in silence for a while, both of our ears tuned in to the sound of sirens.

He couldn't have wanted me to have any. That was clear. There was a certain weakness in his voice when he said it. But, he was sincere, and I wasn't about to complain, thrusting open the bag in my lap and taking out two cans. I didn't hesitate a second, popping open the lid with my good hand, choking on the contents as I forced it down my throat as fast as I could. The beer taste was average compared to everything else, but I never really drank for the taste. Not truly. In many ways, I preferred the hard alcohol because it didn't really taste like anything at all except for icy fire.

"I'm sorry if I made you think I didn't want you to get it out." Nicky suddenly said.

"Oh, I didn't-"

"I'm just worried about you. I feel this strange desire to protect you. Not to say you're fragile, but that shit in the Shell was a lot. It's understandable you'd want to drink. To get high and forget. I want it, too. It's just that...I can see what it does to your mind. You just totally disappear. Not in a normal way. I know what that looks like. My dad drank. He died from alcohol poisoning."

I couldn't speak. That was the last thing I expected him to say.

"It never used to bother me when my friends drank or even when I drank. But, for some reason, I don't know, you're different than all them. I'm just scared for you."

I felt so utterly embarrassed. I knew I had a problem. I knew I didn't drink like other people drank, and Nicky wasn't the first to point that out. And to think now that was another burden I was lacing upon him. He didn't deserve to feel the weight of my fucked up brain after all I put him through. It wasn't fair. It hurt my heart. But it wasn't enough to keep me from wanting more.

I didn't know what to say, so I just pressed the sharp lip of the can back to my mouth.

"Here, give me some of that."

Nicky took the beer from my hands, lifting it up to his own mouth to take a long drink. He wiped his lips with the back of his hand when he'd finished, moaning against his skin.

"Damn, that's good." he groaned with a wide smile on his face as if he hadn't just shared something incredible personal and vulnerable about himself.

I laughed at him without meaning to. At first it was a silly little giggle, but then it erupted into uncontrollable heaving guffaws. I couldn't control it, and I had no idea why. Maybe I was laughing at him. Maybe myself. Maybe at this fucked up situation we were in. Regardless of what exactly it was about, it felt good. So good to laugh and laugh and laugh. Nicky began laughing at me after a minute, then we both couldn't stop.

After a while, we were both gasping for breath. It was amazing to have a genuine smile on my face. And the good kind of tears. With fingers like feathers, Nicky wiped them from my eye, clearing what was left of my runny mascara. I watched as a single teardrop fell into his palm, running down along the lines in his hand. He grinned heavily, his eyes on me, then brought it to his lips to lick it.

"Tastes like venom."

"Venom???"

"Yeah. Your tears are like your venom. It's poisoning to watch."

I could feel the truth in that even if I didn't believe it.

"Sorry if that was weird. I just feel like I know you even though I know nothing about you at all."

I could feel my mouth curving upwards without my consent. To hide the strange feeling I felt in the pit of my stomach that was now rising up and escaping through my face, I cracked open the second can.

"Nah, you're fine. We've been through a lifetime of trauma together. Makes sense." I mumbled, trying to sound indifferent even though it made me feel so good.

"So, you think we're friends?"

"Yeah?"

"I like that."

I took another gulp. "So, tell me. No dad, right? You have a mom? Step-dad?"

I wasn't sure if the question was insensitive, but Nicky only laughed. "Yep. My mom's okay. Step-dad is what you can expect. I've got a little sister though. I love her a lot."

"What's her name?"

"Sophía."

"That's pretty."

"I think so. What about you?"

"Hmm?"

"Any siblings? Parents?"

Filling the gap of silence, I swallowed another massive sip, lifting the can higher and higher above my head as it got lighter. By the time I'd set it down again, it was trickling down my chest, gushing too fast for my mouth to handle. I mopped it up with my sleeve messily, avoiding Nicky's gaze.

"You don't wanna hear about me." I finally managed to get out, rolling down my window to let in a booming current of wind.

"But, what if I do?" Nicky practically shouted, leaning his head over to me.

In an attempt to avoid him, I turned up the radio louder, feeling the bass of the stereo beneath my feet. *Seventeen* by Ladytron was playing; a favorite of mine.

"I love this song!" I cried, rising up on my seat, moving closer to the window.

With no thoughts in my head, I stuck myself out the window, letting the raging breeze catch my hair. I tipped out farther and farther, rocking my back against the door. I stretched my arms far above my head, belting out the lyrics. Stupid yet distracted.

I didn't necessarily feel unsteady, but I suddenly felt Nicky's hands on my waist. I could tell from the gentle brush of his skin that he'd taken one of my belt loops and hooked his finger around it. He brought me such a silly sense of security in everything he did. I knew I wasn't so much as a smidge deserving of it. Of him.

"Kas, be careful!"

The sunset was beginning, bright rays blinding me as we drove into the light. We rounded a turn and suddenly the sun was behind us, warming my jacketed back. I looked out at my hands above me, watching my fingers as they danced against the backdrop of the trees.

I noticed with a bit of pain that these weren't the same hands as a few days ago. These were the hands of a murderer. The thought of it drew me back into the car, the brief high disappearing with the brightness of the day. I wasn't always the most self-aware person, but as more time went on, the more I realized just how badly I'd messed up.

Nicky noticed my sudden change, but didn't press me. He simply rested his hand that had been holding me to safety on my knee, his fingers lightly touching me. His hands were no different than they'd been yesterday or the day before. He hadn't killed someone.

The song ended, switching to another, but hearing the music wasn't making me feel any better. I turned it off with an air of frustration, then rested my head back onto my chair, turning my face away from Nicky. The tears began again and not happy this time. I thought I was quiet enough to keep his attention away, but his sudden grasp of my hand told me otherwise. He didn't bother to wipe my tears or say anything to cheer me up. He only held me still while I began to shake with sobs. His touch was enough to soothe me into only a gentle cry, which was lucky because if I had been sobbing loudly we wouldn't have heard the piercing ding on the dashboard, signaling the car's malfunction.

"What?" Nicky grumbled, pulling us over beside the highway.

I sat up, straining my neck to get a look at what he'd seen. The check engine light was blinking, dinging in time with the flashes. I stepped out of the car before Nicky did, rounding the front, then lifting the hood with a pull of a lever. As I opened it, a huge blast of thick black smoke flushed out at me, sucking the air from my lungs. I coughed breathlessly, backing away until I bumped into Nicky, who was just behind me.

"Damn it." I groaned.

"What?"

"I've had this car forever and they told me it needed an entirely new engine. I couldn't pay for it at the time, so I just didn't do anything about it. It's probably completely fried."

"I don't really know anything about cars. You really think it's unfixable?"

I hesitated before revealing something about myself. "My grandpa was a mechanic. I do know a bit about cars. I might be able to fix it if I had the tools, but I don't have anything with me."

"What do we do then? We're probably a good thirty minutes to Kennewick still."

"Hold on." I sighed, reaching myself forwards towards the engine.

My hands moved out beyond where my eyes could see, feeling around for anything broken or dislodged. I really should've known not to do that, but I was scared and hopeless, trying to save the last bit of protection we had.

"AHH!" I immediately screamed, having burned the back of my good hand on part of the engine.

The hot metal practically melted into my skin, sizzling against my flesh. I coughed through the smoke, my eyes on fire as I wrenched my hand up to my chest, shouting profanities to keep myself from crying out. Nicky tried to reach forward to help, but I shook him off, flexing my fingers to see the damage. It was a small burn and would probably leave a sizable welt, but I was going to be fine. I was only stupid and ashamed.

Determined to move on from my failure, I offered a different solution with so much fatigue and dejection in my voice I almost couldn't tell the words were my own. "There's an exit a mile and a half from here. We could walk and take a bus?"

Nicky hesitated, almost waiting for me to explode like a bomb. "Yeah. Okay," he finally said. "Let's get your stuff from your car, then."

By himself, I watched him walk back around the car, taking out my backpack and the jacket I'd taken off a second before, handing me the latter once we met back at the front. I slipped it over my shoulders, then grabbed the hair tie I remembered leaving in one of the pockets. With a motion I'd performed thousands of times throughout my life, I twisted my hair up into a high pony, cringing a bit at the grease and crusted blood I felt beneath my fingers. Nicky's eyes studied me, looking for words on my lips he knew I wouldn't dare say.

Instead I said, "Ready?"

He nodded, taking the first step into the gravel.

Even though it was probably the greater half of 9 o'clock, there were many cars still shooting down the highway like bullets. With our dark clothing, I knew most of them wouldn't see us, and if they did, it wouldn't be long enough to stop. I figured we were lucky that was the case. It meant we still had to walk over a mile, but at least we didn't risk running into someone we shouldn't have.

I took note of Nicky's pace. Being a whole head and a half taller than me, he walked with a firm solid stride, which I could tell he shortened for me. It was almost painful to watch him take shorter steps, his feet landing stiffly on the ground with his effort. He kept his hands in his pockets, looking out ahead of us. Although, I knew he couldn't have seen much of anything.

"Kasi, hold up." Nicky suddenly whispered, stretching out one of his arms to stop me.

At first, I didn't understand his reason for stopping us, but then, almost impossibly, as headlights began to grow around us, illuminating the gravel, I realized someone was pulling over. By the time I understood what was happening, the door to the car was slammed shut and the sound of heavy footfalls walking towards us filled my ears.

"You folks alright?" a man's deep voice rang out.

I turned and could only see his silhouette against the harsh lights. The jangle of handcuffs on his belt and the murmur of radio chatter, however, told me everything I needed to know about who this man was even if I couldn't see a badge.

"Yes, sir, we're just heading into town, our car broke down a little ways back." Nicky explained, talking with much more ease than I would've been able to.

"I saw. Do you mind just showing me your license and registration for the vehicle real quick? Just want to keep tabs on the car and make sure it gets towed."

The officer moved closer to us, pulling a flashlight out of a back holster. He held it up, shining it into our faces. He only glanced at my face for a second, but his eyes lingered on Nicky, scanning him up and down.

"Sir, I think I might've left my card in-"

"What's your name, son?"

"Um-"

Nicky took a step back as the cop closed in, pointing the flashlight further into Nicky's face so he could barely see. Slowly, as the recognition hit him, the officer shifted on his heel, directing the light into my face, too. I squinted from the brightness of it, trying to keep myself looking as innocent as possible.

"You're Kasandra Walt. Don't move either of you. You're under arrest."

Nicky reached out and grabbed my hand, yanking me into the ditch beside the highway and into the darkness.

"HEY! Stop!"

I couldn't see more than two feet in front of me, but I kept my legs moving. From the sounds I could discern behind me, the officer had begun chasing us, and it sounded like he had called for backup as well. Nicky's guidance was all that kept me from collapsing, and I felt like I had no choice but to fully trust him.

Once we'd climbed up onto the other side of the ditch, we started a mad dash towards the exit that would lead us into town. Sprinting at full speed, we ran along the highway, feeling flashlights shaking across our backs. Sirens began wailing the further we ran, but that only fueled the rage in our legs, pushing us onward. There were streetlights ahead, surrounding the exit ramp, so we crossed back over the ditch, climbing our way up the incline.

Blue and red lights approached us from behind, following us upwards. We didn't have time to stop and talk about where to go, but we both seemed to know the right course of action. We both knew we had to stay off the roads, so hurriedly we ran towards the guardrail across the road at the top of the ramp that ran perpendicularly over the highway. Jumping it and dropping onto the wet grass beyond, we continued onto a dirt path that led into the trees.

"THERE!" a voice shouted.

The officers that'd pursued us in the police cars were catching up, and I could hear them throwing their heavy bodies over the guardrail in our wake. I turned my head for just a moment to see them, not watching where my feet were and tripped over a rock. I splayed out spread-eagle onto the ground, scuffing my hands and knees. The force of my fall kicked up dirt from the path, filling my mouth and eyes. It was all I could do to keep myself from making a sound, so I bit my inner cheek in my effort.

"Shit, Kasi!" Nicky gasped, jogging back to lift me up.

He practically threw me back onto my feet, taking me by the arm as his feet took off. I felt disoriented as we started running again, trying my best to brush the nastiness out of my mouth. I spit a few times onto the ground to dispose of it, catching the taste of blood from having seriously chomped down on my cheek.

The path we were on curved suddenly, turning us back towards the direction of the town. As we got farther and farther from the highway, the trees began to thin and the moon allowed us to see more and more. The more open the space became, the more I could hear the many pairs of feet following us, calling for us to stop. My heart beat furiously in my chest, but I begged myself not to panic. We were experiencing the worst possible case scenario, and I couldn't let Nicky down now.

"Nah, fuck this!" Nicky whined, drawing us up to a chain link fence that was at least nine feet tall.

As the woods faded into urban area, there were abandoned buildings littered around everywhere. The ones we'd approached butted up against tall, metal fencing, most likely intended to keep people like us out. From where we stood, I could see numerous traces of squatters; fire burns, nests of garbage as beds, and old bottles and trash bags. Apart from those things, the entirety of the building had been graffitied. Windows were smashed, siding had been ripped off, and doorways no longer held any doors.

I couldn't tell where the fence ended, but I assumed it went on for a while if it had been put up to prevent people from getting in. We had a few options. But the problem was, we didn't have a lot of time. I listened closely to the sound of our pursuers and noticed I heard the rattle of dog collars, too, and most definitely the "search" command, although faint, given.

"Nicky, we have to go over it." I decided, removing his hand from my arm and walking up to the base of the fence.

"We can't mess this up, okay? If one of us falls, it's over."

"I know that. But, if we don't climb, it's over, too."

We both looked at each other for a second, and I tried to find confidence in his expression. Where there usually would have been a quiet determination, all I could see was fear. It wasn't possible for me to help him, so I did the only thing I could, and I shoved the toe of my shoe into one of the links. My hands rose up high above my head, reaching for the farthest link I could grab. I was careful to use only my fingertips on the injured hand, but it was difficult to keep my balance.

The cold metal scalded my skin as I climbed, pressing deep into my hands. The further up I got, the unsteadier the fence became; rocking and folding inward as my bodyweight moved it. I didn't dare stop or slow my pace, though, because I knew every second I wasted here was a second longer for the police to catch up to us. It occurred to me then that in addition to tracking dogs, the officers might have reason to pull a gun on us. According to them, I still had the murder weapon with me and that classed me as armed.

I breathed in and out in a panting fashion as if I were in labor contracting. The fear in my mind was beginning to take over my body, and I realized I didn't have much time left before it began to shut down entirely.

Fortunately, I was almost at the top, and after a few more lifts, my hands graced the metal beam that lined the topmost part of the chainlinking. I took a moment to look for Nicky before throwing my leg over the other side, and I saw that he was right behind me, climbing just a few feet to my left. He caught me watching him and urged me on, glancing behind us to see if we'd been spotted yet.

"Just go, Kasi."

I didn't hesitate, beginning my descent, recklessly fast. I was much less careful going down than I was going up, and I nearly lost my footing a few times. I managed to hold it together until the halfway point when I chanced a look back through the fence and saw them.

Through the metal links, there were a dozen officers with three different dogs, all holding bouncing flashlights, bursting from the trees.

"Nicky, jump!" I screamed, throwing myself backwards and falling the remaining five feet or so to the ground.

I landed on my feet, but collapsed to the side from the force of the drop, hitting my ribs against the hard ground. All the breath in my body was flushed out of my lungs at the impact, and I laid there gasping as Nicky flung himself down from an even higher height than me. With gingerness, I sat up, crawling over to Nicky, who was trembling on his knees. Together, we helped each other stand, then began a slow jog towards the row of abandoned buildings.

We made it to the cavity of a doorway, racing through the hallway it led into and exiting out the other side. I didn't know if we'd been seen running inside, so I made us cross the street to another multi level building in the same condition. I figured if we had at least one building of protection between us, we'd have enough time to escape if we had been seen.

Once we'd darted into the second building and up a flight of stairs, we took a breath, both of us heaving with exhaustion and lack of oxygen. The room we'd entered was almost completely empty, stripped clean of whatever had once been here. I imagined it might have been an office at some point, but the walls and floors were concrete, all covered in graffiti. There were windows on all sides of the level, but only some were intact. We were lured to one where the glass wasn't cracked and sat down below it to hide. Before we sat down, though, we brushed the sight clear of needles and cigarette butts.

"I can't believe that just happened." Nicky sighed, stretching out his legs in front of us.

We sat side by side underneath the windowsill, which provided a bit of light from the moon. I hugged my legs to my chest, my eyes stuck on the staircase, listening closely for any sound of the cops. Both of us were shaking so desperately, I couldn't tell where most of the movement came from. Awkwardly, I put my hand out and patted Nicky's shoulder, unsure of how else to calm him. There was nothing good to say. Nothing positive to make the moment better.

Except. There was.

"I can't believe I made us jump down." I laughed, finding something funny in the ridiculousness of it all.

"What?" Nicky asked, almost incredulous that I had the gall to make a joke out of it.

"Like, I was lagging behind that whole time, then I just said 'fuck it, lets jump.'"

Nicky shook his head, but I could see a smile on his face. "Alright, idiot, just be quiet."

I giggled under my breath, shaking my head at my own madness.

Chapter 6

"Kasi, wake up. It's your turn to watch."

Nicky shook my shoulders, jolting me awake rather unelegantly. I lifted my head from his shoulder, reminding myself where we were while my eyes adjusted to the darkness. A chill brushed my cheeks, a slight breeze flowing through the building from the broken windows. Glass and garbage littered the floor all around us, save the small space we were curled into.

I pressed my palms to the floor to adjust myself into a more upright position. Beside me, Nicky yawned, stretching himself out a bit and leaning backwards. I watched him out of the corner of my eye, my chest tightening in panic as he began to drift off. He was much smarter and braver than I was. Our agreement to take shifts to sleep and watch until morning was a correct one however incompetent I believed myself to be. If I were to see anything, what would I even do? Run? Scream? I definitely wouldn't do the correct thing on the fly. I'd do the rash thing and possibly get us into more danger. It was no secret that I was a danger myself.

The more time passed, the better my vision became. It was a combination of the moon rising higher in the sky as well as my eyes altering themselves to see in just a touch of light. I studied the large room, trying to be proactive and "less dangerous", searching for possible escape routes or places to hide. The only way out, apart from a two story drop onto concrete, was back the way we came, which meant that if someone were to come up those stairs, we were trapped.

There were, though, many places to hide. Unclean as they most likely were, there were several upturned mattresses and black garbage bags filled with who knows what; things that remained after the squatters had left. I was sure we could hide under a mattress or two or even use the garbage bags as a distraction, throwing them at whoever came up the stairs. It wasn't a good plan, but it was better than acting foolishly if something did happen.

I sighed aloud without thinking about Nicky and he shook a bit, inhaling a sharp gasp before realizing it was only me. Sleepily, he threw his hood over his head, tucking his hands into his pockets. It only took another few minutes for him to drift back to the soft sleep he'd been in, and I vowed to remain quiet, easing my breaths to keep them silent.

Nicky's legs were spread out in front of him, his shoes shining with the bloody remnants of the past. They were messy and dirt riddled just like many of the art pieces around us covered in the dust and grime of time. Most of the graffiti seemed to hold no true significance. Just shapes and squiggles and lines going nowhere. There were large writings of profanities against the wall furthest from me, whispering across the room rather than yell as I'm sure the artist intended. To be fair, those weren't the only words painted around the room. I noticed many "freedom"s and "justice"s and even one "fuck the norm", which I counted as both a profanity and artistic protest.

My eyes moved back around the room, looking for more I hadn't seen. Then, I saw something that confused me. Next to "fuck the norm" was a very big blur of colors that I'd taken to be just shapes and lines before. Now having a second look at it, I realized it was an abstract sunset painted along with what seemed to be a sunrise. Both versions of the sun were equal, but one was regarded with darker colors and more ragged edges. My first thought was some political reference to the social bad and good, but then I saw, in the faintest paint, the words "everything ends".

It was fatalistic in nature, but I didn't think a place like this, given everything else around, that that was the message intended. In relation to the suns, it could mean the day ends, the light ends and the darkness consumes. But, that also meant, the night ends and the light consumes. It went both ways. The good ends, but also the bad.

It was hard to believe, being in our situation, that the bad would ever end. The future was terrifying to think about. My mind dawdled. Always landing back on the vampiric thirst for another drink to distract my mind from its dangerous dawdling. It was an easy out. I couldn't have that now, though. I had to keep watch. If not for myself, then for Nicky.

So dawdle my mind did. Every little rustle of wind or shifting of the trash bags around us, scared me shitless. My stomach churned with the anticipation of the worst, my head splitting open, bursting with thoughts of how maliciously we could both die.

I could catastrophize it so well. I could make myself feel the thump of steps as officers raced to our location, dogs in hand. I saw all of them so vividly, stomping across the room, keys and handcuffs jangling in belts. Some would be out of shape and out of practice huffing from the effort, but others would be quicker. Eventually, they'd reach us. The dogs first. The rough growls and tearing of flesh played like static in my ears. When I closed my eyes, I could feel blood dripping down my body as I screamed for Nicky. It would be too late, though. An officer would have grabbed him, baton in hand, preparing to beat him across the chest. He would struggle, but he would not win.

Neither of us would win. I would succumb to injuries sustained by the dog attack and Nicky would suffer a punctured lung. If he survived, they'd drag him away, putting him in the back of a truck, hauling him away for a murder he didn't commit.

I could picture myself, draped across the floor, laying in a pool of my own blood, watching him leave. My lips would feel the warmth of the liquid beneath me while my eyes would focus on Nicky, shouting loudly, flailing, reaching out for me. (I flatter myself even in my imagination that he would.) Then, I'd die. My eyes would freeze over and dry, my lips would crack, my body would grow limper and limper and eventually the bleeding would stop.

I blinked. The sun was rising. The night had ended and I'd been tucked away in my own mind for most of it. It took a lot of strength to draw myself from the depth of my head, but I did. I felt as if I was in a whole new world. Everything looked different. The light from the East made the room less threatening, made the darkness not as prominent on my chest.

A solitary tear trickled down my cheek and I quickly wiped it away. I had been silly. None of those horrible worse case scenarios were going to happen. I was irrational. I was sober.

"Nicky?" I whispered, tapping his arm, gently.

He hadn't moved much at all from when he'd fallen asleep apart from his legs, which he'd crammed up underneath him. He woke abruptly, turning to meet my gaze with a straight face. Just like it had for me, it took him a couple of moments to realize where we were. When he did, he became more alert, stretching his shoulders backwards and sitting up straighter.

"It's morning already?" he wondered, turning to look out the window behind us.

"Yeah."

"Why didn't you wake me earlier? We agreed on two hour shifts."

"I wasn't tired."

"Did you see anything?"

Even if I'd been conscious enough to notice, I wasn't going to tell him if I had. I had a feeling he would've been upset at me for not waking him.

I shook my head.

"Let's wait a little then until it's lighter, then we can start heading to that town you mentioned."

A couple hours later, we gathered our things and left. We were still early enough in the day that the coming search party had yet to arrive. We'd escaped capture once again, but we couldn't count on that lasting forever. So, with emotional and physical exhaustion plaguing us, we ventured onward. I couldn't pinpoint exactly where we were anymore. I knew the route into town from the highway, but from the abandoned buildings? I had no clue.

"Do you know where we're going?" Nicky asked me as we trudged around the dead overgrown grass that surrounded the buildings.

We weren't about to climb the chain link fence again, so we opted to take the long way around, going past a fence similar to the one we'd thrown ourselves over the night before. The height was even more impressive in the light, towering over us as if the fence itself was one of the buildings.

"No fucking clue. It seems like the woods clear a bit farther this way, so I guess there?" I told him, pointing ahead of us.

Any roads that had once led to these buildings would've been covered in grass and debris by this point, so even if we had found one, it would be hard to navigate. It was incredible how neglected this place was. It was kind of beautiful in a way, though. How nature had started to take over, reclaiming what had once belonged to it.

"You said you've been here before, right?"

I shook my head. "Not here-here. I've been to this town, though."

"Is it busy?"

"Not usually. Kind of the dead sort of pit-stop you'd expect."

"When we make it there, we'll have to keep our heads down and move fast."

"I agree."

I could sense Nicky shudder next to me as we walked side by side in the general direction of civilization. I didn't know if it was a shudder of fear, exhaustion, or maybe even cold. I did know, however, that I had nothing of substance to offer him. Nothing to ease him. So, instead, I slid my arm under his, pulling him to my side so we moved as a unit. He was tense all over, rigidly thrusting his feet forward, almost forcing himself to walk. I tried to relax myself, hoping he could mimic me. It wasn't easy, but eventually, I did. And so did he.

"Kasi-"

"It's okay. I know."

He looked down at me, but I refused to meet his eyes. I was scared of the pain I'd see in them and subsequently feel in my own heart. I couldn't bring myself to face it just yet. I was too sober for that.

"Hey, what's that?" I shouted, catching something dark up ahead of us.

Nicky released me, jogging ahead. I struggled to follow, but a burst of energy swept through me once I realized what we were running to. Somehow we'd managed to find a roadway. A real roadway. With yellow lines and white edges and concrete and everything. I had no way of knowing what road this was or where it would lead, but just the discovery of something as real and tangible as an escape was exciting.

"Which way should we go?" Nicky asked, walking straight out into the center of the closest lane.

"Maybe this way?" I pointed to my right, seeing a wind up ahead that appeared to turn towards my general idea of the town.

"Alright."

With the sun rising behind us, we started along the road, walking close to the treeline in case we needed to dip inside to hide. We must've missed the early morning commuters' rush hour, so we found ourselves in a grace period of little to no traffic. The only cars that passed were going too fast to recognize us anyway, zooming along on their way.

Yesterday, when we ditched the car and ran for it, I heavily underestimated how far of a walk it would be. I thought we could make it into town within an hour, and even now, I believed we were closer. The problem was, no matter how far we walked, we never seemed to make any progress. The trees were gradually thinning, yes, and the road continued onwards as if it went somewhere, but hours went by and we were nowhere near where I thought we'd be at this point.

Our path was hilly and both of us were exhausted. Neither of us could speak more than a few words at a time with all the huffing and puffing we were doing. And, I was beginning to feel sick. I hadn't eaten in so long, or even had anything to drink that wasn't alcohol. My head pounded, my stomach ached, and my skin felt as if it was moving all on its own, burning and tingling with feverish goosebumps. I tried my best to hide it from Nicky, but with his rested, watchful eye he eventually caught on as we came up to a bridge, crossing over some train tracks.

"Let me have the backpack." he offered, holding his hand out for me.

I didn't argue, slinging it off my shoulders and handing it over. I stopped for a second, doubling over with my hands on my knees, trying to breathe gasps of breath quietly through my nose.

Nicky had gone on ahead and when he noticed me not following, called out. "Are you okay?"

I shot up. "Fine! Fine! Just tired."

I moved towards him, finding myself dizzy and disoriented from my abrupt change of position. Nicky noticed this and stood still while I walked straight passed him towards the bridge. I knew he wanted me to turn around and be honest, but I was too embarrassed to be the one who not only got us lost but was also slowing us down.

Halfway across the bridge, I saw an opportunity and hauled myself up onto the ledge.

"Kas! Be careful!"

Nicky's feet began to slap hard against the concrete, running for me.

I swung my legs onto the other side, and I could see clearly below, the dark rusted train tracks leading underneath. Apart from Nicky's stomping, there was silence all around. It was as if everything had stopped, holding still for just a moment. Everything I was feeling was heightened and yet I could separate my mind from it. I could feel all its intensity, but just for a second, I wasn't bothered.

"Kasi, what are you doing?" Nicky's stern voice startled me as he caught up.

"I'm not jumping," I sighed. "Just sitting."

Nicky scanned my face for a lie, but didn't seem to find it. He shook his head after a minute, then climbed up beside me, sitting on the concrete barrier with his feet dangling over the edge like mine. His face sagged with fatigue, but his eyes darted around us like a torpedo, looking for a target.

Immense guilt began to creep up my spine, immediately sending a yearning to my throat and head for something to dissolve it. My first thought was to reach for my backpack on Nicky's back, and I did so without any explanation. He jolted at my hand on his shoulder, but let me slide the straps down his arms so I could bring the bag into my own lap. I opened it, digging through it to find anything to get myself off, realizing how many of the Coors were empty that I thought had been full. It was entirely likely that in my stupor of a "watch" I'd drunk them without thinking.

Then, I remembered.

I twisted the bag around so the front was facing my chest, and I unzipped one of the pockets where a clear plastic bag with a pre-rolled joint was waiting for me. It was only one, but it was big enough to do what I needed it to. To drown me in something other than what I felt.

"You still have that lighter?" I asked, pulling out the Ziploc.

"Here." Nicky pulled his wallet out of one of his pockets and handed me the small red lighter he kept tucked inside.

I pressed the end of the joint to my lips, flicking the lighter on and holding it up to my face. I sucked in a few breaths, making sure it was good and lit, then exhaled heavily, giving the lighter back to Nicky's confused face.

"Kasi, we really shouldn't be in the same place for long."

"You're right. Let me rest a bit, though."

"If you're making us stay here, at least share."

I turned to him, slightly surprised, but handed over the joint all the same. He took a long drag, tilting his head back, his hair fluffing up with his movements. I watched him carefully, recognizing the guilt I felt for putting him in the position that I had, but also admiring him. He was a mystery to me. I knew nothing about him. And, yet, I think a small part of me cared about him. More than a small part, really. He looked so small, sitting there beside me, and I felt a deep longing to protect him.

"That's really good. Did you roll it yourself?" Nicky wondered, giving me back the joint.

"Nah, I bought them like that. I don't smoke very often. I usually prefer a different high."

I spoke before I knew what I was saying. Although, it wasn't like my alcoholism wasn't written all over me in soot-black ink. My self-loathing and reckless regard for my health had become just as much a part of me as the fact that I had brown eyes and chapped lips and hangnails and dry skin.

Nicky mumbled something I couldn't understand, reaching for another drag. We spent the next ten minutes or so taking turns passing the joint to the other, saying nothing while we looked out at the tracks and trees and the rocks and trash that lined the edge of the rails. The more time went on, the more intense the high began to feel. Just like the pain had, the high seeped into my skin, reaching my very core, reaching a hand in and gripping my organs.

"You know how I told you I have a sister?" Nicky suddenly said, placing his hand down beside me and shifting himself into a more relaxed position.

"Mhm."

"She's like my best friend. I mean, like, we fight a lot like siblings, but I love her more than anything. I don't think she knows I do. I kinda wish I would've told her, y'know?"

"You'll get to."

Nicky's eyes found mine. "Maybe. I hope she becomes a better person than I am. I hope she picks the right friends, goes to school, gets out of Oregon. She's obsessed with fanfiction. She never writes it herself, but she loves drawing the characters she reads about. I've seen some of her sketches and they're actually really good. I always wished that I could be good at something like that. Or good at anything, really. She's so kind and everyone adores her. A lot of people are rude to her, but I can see the jealousy so clearly. Compared to her, I'm a miserable excuse for a person."

"Don't say that."

"You don't know me, Kasi. I'm her older brother and I'm supposed to be the role model and the good boy and someone who she can be proud to call family. I haven't done anything of value in my life. Not a damn thing."

"You saved me."

Nicky shied away from my stare, pretending to scratch his face on his shoulder.

I didn't know what to say. It hurt me that he thought of himself that way. The truth was, though, I thought the same thing about myself. I know what he would do if I said something like that. If I degraded myself to nothing more than worthless nothingness, he would be furious. And for what reason? I didn't deserve it.

"Nicky-"

I was cut off from my sorry excuse for empathy by a gentle meowing from behind us. We both whipped our heads around to find a small, black kitten with big green eyes staring at us from the sidewalk. The little cat was dirty, thin, and so deeply precious it made me instantly want to cry.

"Where did you come from?" I whispered, lowering myself from the bridge wall to kneel beside the creature.

It walked straight for my hand, not afraid of my large presence at all, and curled up against my palm. Nicky squatted beside us, extending a hand out to stroke the kitten's back with a few fingers. It was shaking like mad and was cold to the touch. With no thought to diseases or rabidness, I scooped it up off the ground and cradled it to my chest. Nicky leaned in close, blowing on the cat's face. He then wiped the gunk from around its eyes, using only the lightest touch from his thumb.

"What is it?" he asked.

I held the kitten up so its belly was showing.

"A girl."

"Awww, sweet little thing." I cooed.

"Do you think she has a mama?"

"I hope she wasn't hit by a car or something."

Both our heads were drawn to the road, looking around as if the body of a cat would magically appear in front of us. There were no signs of anything around the bridge. No more kittens. No mother. Dead or alive.

"What should we do with it?" Nicky wondered, holding his hands out to take the kitten from me.

I handed it to him and grabbed my backpack from the bridge wall. "Let's take it with us. Just until we can leave it somewhere safe."

"I'm fine with that." he said with a smile, bringing the kitten closer to his chest.

My heart fluttered at his attentiveness. All the gentility he'd shown towards me was not exclusive to people. He sheltered it like a glass vase, holding it firm enough not to drop it, but soft enough to not crack its delicateness. I realized as my heart went from a flutter to an ache that I longed for someone or something to treat me that way. Alcohol was violent and it hurt. It wasn't really a comfort the way what I was seeing was. It was like ibuprofen. You take it once, then six hours later you take it again because the effect wore off.

Nicky's eyes were glued to the tiny black head in his arms, so he couldn't see me enamored by him. I shrugged the dead look off my face and spun away, marching across the bridge and further down the road.

If before we had only shared a few words, now we were dead silent. Nicky was locked onto the kitten, and I was doing everything in my power to keep from retching up all the bile in my stomach. I kept myself focused on the yellow lines in the center of the pavement, watching them closely until they blurred. We took so many odd turns with no intersecting streets, I was beginning to fear we weren't going in the right direction at all, hopelessly lost without luck of anyone, even the police, finding us.

But, just when I found myself wanting to give up and just as the sun was nearly set on another day, the trees dropped off in the way that manmade deforestation does. We'd somehow made our way back towards the highway, taking a parallel path without knowing it. We were just a small field from the whooshing cars and a bright green exit sign that read "next exit 1 mile".

"Nicky, I know where we are!" I shouted, jogging down the ditch beside the road.

Chapter 7

I could hear Nicky's footsteps trailing me, and I led the way as we rushed across the harvested field and to the road sign. Once under it, we walked straight through and followed the traffic the remaining mile to the exit. We had really gotten off track only moving by way of the backroads. We must've entirely circled back on ourselves, looping around to the exit we'd originally been chased up. It was lucky, honestly, that the area was so deserted, and it was eerie that it was. We'd only just been here, sprinting in a panic, and now there was no trace that a chase had ever happened.

Darkness fell quickly, and I was only able to see once we got nearer to the exit, home to a few streetlights, towering ominously along the ramp. We trudged up it, feeling the impact of the incline more than we would in a car. At the top, we took a right, heading downhill again towards the bright lights of the strip and away from the guardrail we'd jumped over last night. Restaurants, gas stations, liquor stores, and most importantly, a bus station met us; a much prettier sight than the dark maze of woods just beside it.

I recognized this area from driving back and forth to work, so I knew immediately where to go. I guided us past a McDonald's and behind a Sunoco, taking a shortcut through an alleyway to the bus station on the other street. There were no buses sitting outside at the moment, but the lights on the inside of the building told me they must still be open. Surely, we could find a bus going somewhere. Anywhere. And soon.

"Hey, look." Nicky laughed, pointing farther down the sidewalk as we were about to enter the main sliding doors.

I turned to where his finger led and saw a lone hot dog cart, sitting underneath the bus station awning, its stainless steel exterior practically glowing under the fluorescent light. The young, bearded guy working there seemed to be closing up for the night, but he hadn't yet locked up the top.

"We haven't eaten anything in a long time. I'll go get us some?"

"What about the cat?"

"I'll see if this guy knows where I can take her."

"Do you need money?" I asked, reaching towards my backpack.

"Nah, I've got some," he smiled, patting his back pocket. "Take your wallet to get the tickets, though. I'll pay you back later."

"Are you kidding? I'm not letting you pay for the tickets." I grinned, taking out my wallet.

"Alright. Alright."

Nicky shook his head, his smile so contagious. He had no reason to smile. Neither of us did, really, but it was hard to look at his face and feel nothing. The absence of terror for a couple hours had had an impact on him, and I was starting to feel it, too, through him.

The sound of the sliding doors opening with a squeal forced me to look away from him. A man in tight leather pants strode out from in front of me, only taking a quick glance at me from the side. I followed his path backwards into the station, walking directly up to the woman at the counter, typing away at a keyboard.

"How can I help you?" she groaned with monotony. It was clearly the end of her shift.

"Are there any buses going out tonight?" I wondered, trying my best not to sound wretchedly desperate.

"Matter of fact, yes, hun. There's one going to Kennewick. It'll be here in half an hour or so." The tone in her voice had changed. I must've sounded more desperate than I thought.

"That's perfect. Thank you. I need two tickets."

"Was that your boyfriend out there?"

I didn't feel like speaking any longer than I had to, so the lie was easy. "Yep. We're heading back to school."

"Are you guys at the University?"

"Mhm."

She started to wring the tickets up. "My daughter's there. She's in her first semester of her sophomore year."

I showed my teeth in a fake smile, not quite knowing how to respond.

"That'll be $55, darling."

I nearly took out my credit card, then remembered it might be being tracked. Instead, I handed her three 20's, grateful that I hadn't forgotten to restock my cash supply. She passed me my change in the same hand she held the tickets, her wrinkled skin touching mine briefly.

"You be careful, sweetheart. Make it back to school safe."

The woman's initial hostility towards me had completely melted away. Part of me wondered if I reminded her of her daughter, but that thought was too unsettling to think about. I had no idea who that woman was or who her daughter was, but I could without a doubt guarantee we were nothing alike. I was a hot mess of a human. And I'd done a despicable thing.

I did my best to smile with sincerity, spinning on my heel and walking straight back outside. There was plenty of seating inside the station, but I couldn't stand to be still anywhere for long. Ever since we'd left my car and truly long before that, I'd been so anxious to keep moving.

As I turned the corner, I could see Nicky talking and laughing with the man at the hotdog cart, holding one in either hand. The hotdog man held the kitten in his arms, stroking its back with slow sweeping motions. There were smiles on both of the mens' faces, so I knew there was nothing to fear as I walked down towards them, offering to carry one of the hotdogs for Nicky.

"Here," he breathed, lowering one into my open palms. "Thanks again." he nodded back towards the man.

I nodded gratitude towards him as well, realizing as the warm, thick scent of the hotdog in my hand wafted up to my nose that I was in fact starving. Drinking as much as I had without anything to eat had taken a toll on my strength. It was a miracle I'd been able to walk at all, let alone miles here. Though my legs shook with weakness, I didn't dare sit down. I had to keep moving.

"He's gonna take the cat to a shelter on his way home," Nicky updated me with a mouthful of food as we started walking away. "Although, I think he might be tempted to keep it himself."

I felt a prick of sadness at the loss of our friend, but glad that it would be given a better opportunity to live than we could've provided it with. "That's amazing. What are the chances?

Nicky shrugged, his mouth too full to reply.

"Let's go this way, then," I suggested. "The lady said it should be thirty minutes or so before the bus gets here."

He took another large bite, smearing mustard and ketchup all over his face. The sight of him brought a true chuckle to my lips as I brought my own hotdog up to them. Apart from the occasional mocking of the other, we stayed relatively silent, our footsteps slow to reflect the focus we both had on eating. We both practically swallowed the hotdogs whole, gasping for the food.

I hadn't paid much attention to where we were walking. I only knew it was away from the main roadway. Away from the lights and sounds of late workers driving home. I didn't recognize much around us as I'd usually stuck to the main strip when I came through here before, so I was surprised when we rounded a corner to find a small little shop with an old fashioned tv display out front.

"Oh, my gosh. Look at this." I laughed, stopping in my tracks.

I was shocked not only to find the tvs there, but to also see them on, screening the news this late at night. With the thick glass, the sounds they emitted were faint, but if we leaned in we could hear them. A woman with long, shiny brown hair was just finishing up the weather report, gracefully gliding away from the greenscreen. As she disappeared out of frame, the camera switched back to a man and another woman at a round table both holding papers in their hands.

Thank you so much, Susan. For those of you who missed the previous hour, we have a brief local story or rather warning to send out. We recently got more information about the attack in the Shell, and the police have identified both of the individuals who ran from the scene. The woman, 22 year old Kasandra Louise Walt, who worked at the Shell off of 84 was the one to stab 33 year old Nate West. However, there was a significant scuffle beforehand involving 20 year old Nicky Vargas, who just celebrated his birthday last week. They were discovered to have stayed the night in a motel around Charleston, but are now on the run again. The police urge everyone in the area to remain vigilant and report any information they may have on either individual. They are believed to be armed. Here is footage from the event.

As the words left the man's mouth, the screen switched to security cam footage, blurry and dim, but distinguishable nonetheless. It was odd seeing it replayed from this angle, and I looked so...scary. I was absolutely mad with fear? Anger maybe? I wasn't sure, but it was terrifying. My instinct was to shy away from the crystal clear rendition of my horrible crime, but I couldn't look away. My eyes were glued to the screen, watching it as if it were being replayed in slow motion.

There I was behind the counter, then the fight in the aisles, then Nicky lunging at the man, then me running towards them both, and then...

I felt as if I was about to pass out, but it wasn't me who started to stumble. Nicky fell right into me, tripping over his feet. I grabbed onto him, keeping him steady as he placed both his palms on the glass, heaving sharp breaths. In and out. In and out.

I was so shocked the feeling of nausea left me. I felt so suddenly responsible for Nicky. I could see the physical damage I'd done to him. He shook with grief. This was killing him.

I had an urge to reach out and touch him in a gentler, more intentional way, but I wasn't sure if he'd want that. He might've already changed his mind about sticking with me. At any moment, he could run to the police and turn me in. He could claim self-defense and that I wasn't sober. He could say I'd forced him to run at knifepoint. Regardless of his being Latino, surely there was enough evidence against me for them to at least let him go. He could go on and live his life. It would be so easy.

"Nicky?" I whispered, taking a step closer to him.

"When's that bus coming?" his breath caught, breaking with his attempt at strength. He was crumbling before my eyes.

"Probably ten minutes now?"

"Let's head back. I don't want to be here any longer."

"Are you okay?"

He stared me dead in the face, biting down hard on his lower lip. I wished so much in that moment that I could know what he was thinking.

"C'mon." was all he muttered, marching past me back in the direction of the bus station.

I hadn't realized how far we'd wandered and felt a twinge of anxious eagerness in my stomach as I saw a bus already at the station when we came within sight of it. Luckily, though, it only seemed to have arrived recently, so we didn't run the risk of missing it entirely. Regardless, Nicky upped his pace, forcing me to jog along behind him.

Without speaking, he climbed up before me, stretching his neck around his shoulder to make sure I was still following. I grabbed onto the greasy handrail, stepping up onto the high, rubber laced steps after him. My heart was pounding still, but I knew more than ever how important it was to be strong.

He picked a seat in the center of the bus where the least amount of people were. It was a cushioned bench seat; the kind where the fabric of the chair pills with the carpet-like material it's made of. As gross as it might have been, there was a certain coziness to the seat that made it all the more inviting as the night closed in around us.

"Here, put this over your head. Your hair is really noticeable." Nicky whispered, drawing the hood of my jacket up over me.

His fingers lingered just for a moment by my ear, brushing a bit of hair behind it. He focused so intently on hiding the straight strands of brown from my head, I doubted whether he noticed how much I appreciated the tenderness of his touch. I couldn't help smiling at him, and within a second, all the tension of the past fifteen minutes seemed to ease.

"What?" he chuckled, noticing the grin on my face.

I shook my head, feeling my cheeks flush. Although he laughed, I could hear the strain in his voice; the genuine concern he was trying so hard to suppress. I curled my fist up into a ball, pressing it into my cheek to cover my face. I immediately winced at the pain in my palm. There had been so many other things overriding the ache, but now that we sat in silence, I felt it weeping in its hurt. Our makeshift bandage was enough to stem the wailing agony, but it wasn't sufficient in fixing the problem. *My* problem that I had so embarrassingly caused. Even though I wanted to scream out, I sucked in my tongue and shied away from Nicky. I couldn't burden him with this now.

A few more people got on after us, everyone clearly intent on keeping to themselves. I was grateful. I couldn't be sure how many of them had noticed the news or how many of them would bother to heed the police's warning. It put me in the mindset, however, of envisioning everyone as an enemy. It was a good reminder to keep to myself and not look anyone directly in the eye. And I did so until the last person sat down, a muffled speaker announced our departure, and the bus jolted forward with a loud hiss.

Once we left the bright gleam of the bus station, everything went dark. The only light that remained were the few interior bulbs along the footboards of the bus, which dripped a lovely cast of shadows over the entirety of the aisleway. Without the pressure of worrying about the continued arrival of passengers, Nicky let his posture slouch, spreading his legs out and leaning his head against the window. I watched him carefully out of the corner of my eye, finding myself feeling something beyond the usual stabbing of guilt. I wasn't exactly sure what it was I felt, at first, but then, I soon realized.

As we drove down a ramp back onto the highway, a police car going the other way passed us quickly, its lights blaring and siren wailing. Nicky immediately stiffened, his shoulder blades crushing together as his foot began to tap on the floor with agitation. A lone streetlight from a bridge above us illuminated his face for just a second and I could see tears running down his cheeks.

Watching him, seeing for one of the first times how sincerely terrified he must've been, unleashed something in me. It was the same something that kept me from running out of the Shell. The same something that drove me to kill someone. A sense of colossal protectiveness consumed me. I felt this overwhelming, relentless need to make him safe. No matter what it took. And I had no idea why.

He was a stranger to me, and yet, I felt as if I'd known him my whole life.

Once the flash of light hid Nicky's face again in the blackness of the bus, I took his outstretched hand in both of mine, warming it. He looked to me, clear confusion and embarrassment in his eyes, but I only stared back, hoping my face conveyed the empathy I felt. Neither one of us made a sound, nor did we flash a smile. We just sat there, staring.

Tears continued to fall down Nicky's face, slower than they had been a second ago, but flowing nonetheless. I could see so much pain within them. Not rage exactly, but definitely fear.

"Whatever happens," I said, not even sure of what I was about to tell him. "I'll never leave you. I'll be with you. If you want me to."

I wasn't even sure what that meant, but it seemed to instantly have an effect. His face remained still, but his eyes grinned, his fist unclenching in my grasp. I curled my arm under his, cuddling up beside him. I interlocked my left foot with his right one, pressing my hip and thigh into his. He squeezed my arm, then lowered his head onto mine, releasing his weight on me. It was a bit awkward with him being so much taller than me, but it didn't feel wrong for me to hold him as I did. The ball he wound into made him feel so young beside me. Now, I knew how young that was.

"Kasi?" he asked, lowering his lips to my ear.

I inhaled sharply, surprised by him. "Mmm?"

"Thank you."

"For what?"

"For saving me."

"I should be saying that to you."

"You don't understand, though. I feel like you're the only reason I'm still alive."

I blinked heavily, trying to follow. "Nicky-"

"I'm being honest. I am so grateful for you. I've never been afraid of you. Not even for a minute."

"Do you really feel that way?"

"Yes. Kasi, you saved my life by killing him. I'm forever in your debt."

"Nicky, I ruined your life. I ruined my life."

"Stop," there was anger in his voice now. "Just thank you, okay?"

"Okay. You're welcome. You're forever welcome."

Chapter 8

It was nearing ten when we entered the city, its bright lights shifting us from our restful places. Nicky and I had traded spots, so I was closest to the window, although he hadn't released his grip on me. As we exited the highway, Nicky straightened, staring out the window into the now glowing traffic. There were twice as many cars here as there had been in Charleston, and the two lane path that led into the heart of the city beamed with startling red brake lights of the cars ahead of us.

"Are you awake?" Nicky suddenly whispered, taking my hand from my lap.

"Mhm."

"I was thinking. We can't have been the only ones to have seen the last news hour, right?"

"Right."

"People are going to be looking for us."

"Right."

"We're too noticeable, don't you think? We have to hide who we are. Like in the movies."

"What do you mean?"

"Well, we could cut your hair and dye it. Maybe buy some new clothes for both of us?"

"Why dye and cut only mine?"

"Trust me, they're not gonna be looking at my hair too much. Or even me for that matter."

The hint at what he really meant made my chest tighten. They weren't going to be looking at him because he wasn't a murderer. I was far too noticeable for that reason alone.

The bus stop was only another few minutes further into the city, and on the way, we passed a Dollar General and a Goodwill. We decided they would be our best bet for getting new things, partly because of how cheap we expected them to be and partly because they were the only places open.

"Have a good night." the bus driver muttered as we stepped off.

More than ever I was conscious of looking at people, hiding my glance from anyone and everyone we walked passed. I mumbled a reply to the driver, grabbing my hood in my hand, holding it closer to my face. Nicky placed a gentle hand on my back from behind me, guiding me forward in a brisk walk. We immediately ducked out of the light of the bus station, treading onto the dimly lit sidewalk. We kept that quick pace for a block or two before we reached the stores we'd been eyeing.

"DG first?" Nicky wondered, although I wasn't so sure it was a question as much as it was him thinking aloud.

This late at night, the parking lot was nearly vacant, only two cars sat parked beside the building. One small white suv and another big black Suburban. The cars outside matched the people who owned them perfectly; a small old little woman at the cash register and a tall lanky man restocking shelves. I nodded to them as we entered the sliding doors, stepping away from Nicky instantly.

"Let's split up." I whispered, eyeing what the man, who'd been restocking, was next to.

"Alright, I'll get some hair dye." he replied, his head on a swivel looking for where to go.

It was a good thing he was too because I might've been ten times more uncomfortable if he'd noticed what had caught my attention. I hesitated a moment as Nicky hurried off, waiting for the man in the aisle to leave. He had headphones in and was clearly preoccupied, unable to catch me watching him from just a few feet away. He placed the last ice cream container from the top box on his cart in the freezer, shutting it behind him. We crossed each other in the aisle as I made my move, and he didn't acknowledge me at all. I should've been much more worried about him recognizing who I was, but I was just too focused on getting to the next fridge over.

My hands reached out in front of me, masters of my own desire, and wrenched open the cold, foggy door. A blast of frozen air met my face, cooling the sweat off my forehead I hadn't realized had been developing. The cool taste of air made my lips go dry, thirsting for what it was I wanted on the bottom shelf. Corona.

Quickly, I tucked a six pack under my arm, unable to keep my eyes off it. I could practically feel it running down my throat, easing every bit of anxiety I felt. I would've sat down right there and went to town if it hadn't been for Nicky I knew would be waiting for me. The image of disappointment on his face made me cringe in guilt, fearful of his silent understanding I didn't deserve. I knew, deep down, there was judgment behind those beautiful dark eyes. I knew there was judgment behind my own eyes too. But, that was never enough reason to stop.

Light, elevator-style music began playing, emphasizing how empty the store was. It should've made me feel better to know there weren't dozens of eyes on me, but, I just felt uneasy. As if every move I took was being watched.

And it was.

I wasn't sure how long I'd been standing, cradling the Corona like a baby in front of the open fridge, but an awkward cough from the man shook me from my thoughts. He stood, watching me from afar, another box of ice cream in his hand.

"Oh, that's what I was looking for." I laughed, trying to hide my alarm.

I grabbed a tub from his open box, placing it on top of the Corona. He stared at me for a second, trying to find some reason to mark me suspicious, but he didn't seem to. He simply shrugged and got back to work, ignoring me once more.

I bought my findings at the register before I met back up with Nicky, hoping he wouldn't question why I was so obviously hiding the bag of my goodies behind my back. He didn't seem to care, however, as he was much too preoccupied with picking out the right color.

"I don't know, would this look good on you?" he asked, holding the box up to the side of my face.

I moved the bag from my good hand to my bad, flinching as the tight plastic of the bag handle dug into my wrapped hand. Nicky handed the box of stark white blonde to me, then grabbed another, looking intently at the description. I watched him, his lips pursed, his face scrunched up in concentration, his eyes narrowed with determination. It brought warmth to my face seeing his selflessness. But, only for a second. The heavy bag of beer in my hand reminded me of how much I wasn't worthy of it.

"I think we should go platinum. It'll be such a wild change for you; it might even lighten the brown in your eyes. No one could recognize you from a distance."

"Alright. Let's do it, but quickly, I wanna get out of here." I mumbled, letting Nicky walk ahead of me, so he couldn't see my bag.

After we checked out, we stepped next door to the Goodwill. We both picked out a couple outfits of very inconspicuous clothes; a few pairs of low rise, baggy jeans and graphic tees for me and nearly the same for Nicky. The prices were good enough for us to grab some indulgence items too like underwear and a couple bras for me. I was very much looking forward to getting out of the blood stained ones I still wore.

"I saw a motel on the way here," Nicky told me as we walked ourselves out of the Goodwill parking lot. "It's better we're in the city more instead of on the outskirts, I think."

The motel he had seen was only a twenty minute walk from where we were, which, all things considered, wasn't too bad. We booked a room for just one night, not wanting to make any permanent plans. I found I was truly fine with the arrangement, feeling almost safe in what the future would hold. The more we'd distanced ourselves from the past horrors, the more at ease I discovered myself to be. It was odd, but I didn't mind.

I set up a chair in the bathroom as soon as we settled our things, sneaking the pack of beer in there with me as I waited for Nicky.

My fingers fumbled on the lid of the Corona, cracking it open with some force, then tipping my head back to gulp down as much as I could. I could hear Nicky rummaging around in the bags, so I knew I had just a few more seconds to gorge myself. I'd become so self-conscious about drinking in front of him. I didn't need him to approve of me and my actions, but, selfishly, I wanted him to. Hoping the shuffling of the plastic bag was enough to mask my gasps, I took in a huge breath of air, chugging down the rest of the Corona in one large swallow, throwing it into the trash can beside me when I finished.

"Fuck, Kas, I didn't grab any scissors." Nicky grumbled, suddenly stomping his way back into the bathroom with the hair dye box in his hands.

"Sorry." I whispered, knowing it was probably just as much my fault as it was his. I hadn't been very much help.

"It's fine, we'll figure it out."

"Wait," my hands moved forward before my words could follow. "I could make a shiv out of this."

As I held it up in front of him, Nicky's eyes looked straight past it to mine. There was a moment of pain, not quite disappointment, then his gaze returned to its normal friendliness.

"Good idea."

"I'll work on this while you get started?" I offered, tucking the empty can into my lap.

"Sure."

From behind me, Nicky sighed, grabbing a stark white towel off the hook beside the bathtub/shower combo and draping it over my shoulders. With very careful fingers, he took my hair out of the ponytail I had it in, laying it gingerly on top of the towel.

"Alright, I've only ever done this once."

I chuckled. "That's more than I have."

"Really?"

"Yeah, this is my natural hair."

"I'm sorry we have to do this."

"No," I frowned at my reflection in the mirror. Beaten and miserable. "Change is good."

An "uhuh" followed, signaling the end of much conversation. I decided to get to work on the can, bending it and squeezing it to find a weak spot in the metal. The loud popping in my lap distracted me wholly, so I was shocked a little when a cold wetness plopped onto my head.

"Sorry, I know it's cold." Nicky whined, placing a hand at the base of my neck to keep me still.

His warmth was a dramatic contrast to the bleach on my head, smelling like chemicals, feeling like it was melting into my scalp. Naturally, I leaned into him, forgetting whatever insecurity I'd had before.

The bottle emptied onto me with a loud squelch, then both Nicky's hands went to work on me. I could feel him so vividly, spreading the dye around like it was liquid gold; being careful and only making slow, steady movements. His inexperience was obvious, but it didn't matter, his gracefulness made up for it. The coolness of the leather chair I sat in didn't feel so cold anymore with his body so close to mine as he leaned around me to cover every inch. My eyes began to feel heavy in no time, my lids falling closed without my permission.

I could imagine myself, just for a second, somewhere that wasn't here. In a hair salon maybe or perhaps I finally got around to getting the head spa I'd always wanted. Wherever it was, it was pure peace. And Nicky was there. No matter how I looked at it. Nicky was always there.

"Almost done."

Nicky's breath by my ear shook me. My eyes shot open, my fingers instantly continuing to pry open the can. I was careful not to use my injured hand much, but in my efforts, I sliced a finger on the other one as I finally crumpled the can into something that resembled a shiv. I yelped out without meaning to, shoving my finger into my mouth.

"Kasi! Come on!"

"What?" I gasped, almost laughingly.

"What am I gonna do with you?"

"You can't be mad."

"Why not?"

"What is it to you if I get hurt or not?" I heard the ache in my voice as I said it and hoped he didn't hear it as well.

He hesitated. "I just...I dunno. Whatever. Gimme the fucking thing."

I handed him the can, noticing the upset expression on his face. I'd seen this face on him before. It was the same one I'd seen when he'd wrapped my injured hand and held my hair back when I got sick and tackled the man in the Shell. It was a face of angry pain. Not his, but mine.

"The box says we have to let your hair set for thirty minutes, so now might be a good time to use this." Nicky muttered, examining the shiv.

"You're not gonna do it yourself, are you?"

"I was."

Standing up, I took the can out of his hands before our eyes could meet again. "No way. Sit down."

Muttering under his breath, he obeyed, plopping down into the chair with an over exaggeration I didn't think was necessary. I wasn't really worried so much about him, though. I knew I wasn't half as graceful and gentle as Nicky was. I could never have hoped to do half as good a job as he'd done with me so far. Honestly, him doing his own hair would probably be the better bargain, but I just wanted so badly to be useful to him. I owed him so much.

As it was, Nicky's hair was perfect. I hated to ruin it. Long curling ringlets draped his face, framing his cheeks and jawline with a youthful roundness. His dark roots faded into a lighter brunette the farther they fell from his scalp, so I decided to start there. If I could make his hair look entirely dark and if I cut off the most obvious curls, he'd blend right in to every stereotypical man out there.

With my good hand, I gripped one long, thick strand of hair, stretching it out above him. At about exactly halfway on the strand, I placed the edge of the shiv, sawing it back and forth. Where scissors may have cleanly cut, the shiv practically hacked, making the dramatic change in length look wolfy. One glance at Nicky in the mirror and I saw his eyes shut tightly, cringing at what was being done to him.

"I'm no good at this." I apologized.

"No, it's not that. I just hate having my hair cut."

"Oh."

"Yeah. It's weird. I know."

"Why? Did something happen?"

Nicky's eyelids parted and our gazes met in the mirror. I kept my hands working, trying to act busy, but I was deadly curious.

"Um…" the hesitation was obvious. "I mean…it's not so much the act of hair cutting as it is what having shorter hair means."

"That's fair. You shouldn't even have to be here."

"No, that's not what I meant. I mean, yes, neither one of us should have to be here, but I meant that…it's embarrassing."

"You don't have to tell me."

"*I want to.*"

The forcefulness in his voice made me shiver.

"Look, when I was younger my dad…when he would drink…I was always the target of his fury. He never hit me or anything, but he would yell like crazy. Call me things like a pussy and a faggot and an idiot. He would say I was too like my mom. Too sensitive. Too feminine. He hated my hair the most because it was long and curly like hers. He would make me wear a buzz all the time. I never had the courage to fight back. To say anything to him. He would always apologize when he sobered up, but that was never enough. I was never enough for him-"

His words caught, seemingly stuck inside his mouth. His eyes flashed shut again, his face wrinkling up like he was fighting something. I realized it was probably the urge to cry. I placed my hand on his shoulder, squeezing it gently, having no idea what to say.

"When he died, I wanted to be nothing like him. So, I grew my hair out as long as I wanted it. It's not really long, but just long enough so you can see how much it looks like my mom's. I loved my dad. Maybe too much. I was young and just wanted my daddy. No matter how much he hurt me."

Tears began to fall as his memories surfaced, his bottom lip puckering as he held back sobs. I bent down over him immediately, not caring about the mess of hair on his shirt, and wrapped both my arms around his shoulders. I pressed my cheek into his, feeling the tears against my skin. He grabbed onto my wrist in a sudden movement, not to push me away, but to hold onto me. Like I was the only thing keeping him on Earth.

"I'm so sorry, Nicky." I whispered into him.

I couldn't imagine what being with me must be doing to him. Watching me drink, seeing how reckless I am with my life. I know I don't take care of myself. I know what I'm doing is going to one day kill me. I know that. But, that never mattered to me. Not until now. I didn't want Nicky to see his abusive dad in me everytime he looked at me. I couldn't stand to be that. Nicky was far too precious and innocent. Maybe not innocent in experience, but I just knew his heart was good. *He* was good.

But, I couldn't stop. Even as I cradled him in my arms, my eyes beginning to burn from more than just the chemicals in the air and the pain in my hand, I couldn't stop the ridiculous urge to get another drink. To wet my lips, to destroy my stomach. The sting of the burning alcohol would destroy this feeling. This feeling of immense hurt at what Nicky had gone through and was continuing to go through because of me.

A second more passed and the moment was over. Nicky reached up a hand to wipe his eyes and sniffled, pushing me away.

"How close are you to being done?" he asked, averting my eyes.

"Not too much more. I think your hair might curl up after all once it gets wet."

"Alright. You have maybe five more minutes on your hair, then we'll rinse it."

In the time that remained, I did my best to gather the hair on the floor, shoving it into the trashcan under the sink and wiping bits of hair dye that had dripped onto the tile. Nicky simply sat and watched me, playing with his hands, rubbing his palms over and over. Once my hair was ready to be rinsed, he took the chair and moved it out into the bedroom while I placed a few towels on the side of the tub to make it more comfortable. I then sank to my knees while Nicky leaned over me, washing my hair thoroughly with the nozzle attachment.

He was just as gentle as he had been before, working through my hair with the utmost concentration. It was awkward bending over the edge of the tub as I was, but Nicky's care and attention made it all the more worth it.

The last step was to shampoo and condition, using the small, little, slippery bottles that came with the box. Being as slippery as they were, it wasn't a shock when Nicky's wet fingers dropped the conditioner bottle beside me.

"Fuck, I got it." he grumbled, lunging forward.

His knee pressed into me just above my hip, warming the side of my now soaked shirt. As he bent precariously over me, his knee rose, resting just under my breast. I gasped a little in surprise at the feel of him, but I didn't find myself eager to move. My heart frantically beat in my chest, and I prayed that he could not feel it. I didn't know what was happening. I didn't understand this feeling.

"Here." I shouted, reaching for the bottle myself.

As I handed it to him, he sat away, seemingly without having noticed he'd touched me in such a sensitive place. The minute he moved, I wanted him back. I wanted him close to me. It was a dangerous, addictive longing for security. At least, I thought so.

"M'kay. You're all done. I think I'll shower real quick just to get all the hair off, then we'll cut yours." Nicky said, haphazardly, turning off the water.

Before I had a chance to leave, he tore his shirt off over his head, tossing it to the ground beside me. I grabbed it on my way out, tucking it under my arm. Nicky was just about to strip his pants off when I closed the door for him, shouting at him to have some decency. He only laughed.

"You've seen me before. I don't really care!"

"I don't want to see any more than I already have." I yelled back.

His response was only the sound of the water turning back on and the beginnings of steam rushing out the crack in the door.

While I waited for him, I rubbed my hair dry with a towel, looking at my new self in the mirror. It was odd seeing myself so blonde. It was white blonde really. Such an unnatural look for me. Only after a minute, I could sense myself shying away from the mirror and curling up into a ball on the bed. I figured if I didn't look too closely at myself I couldn't see all the damage I'd done. Not only physically.

Nicky's shirt was crumpled next to one of the pillows, and I took it in my hands. It was still heated from being on his body, a little damp from the water, but it smelled like him. Before I truly realized what I was doing, I brought it up to my nose, shoving my face into it. I breathed deeply, allowing my lungs to fill themselves with only his scent. That smell, lately, had become a comfort to me. Whenever Nicky was close to me, I knew that nothing could hurt me. If I could just lock this scent inside me forever, I wouldn't have anything to be afraid of. Even myself.

The sound of the shower suddenly shutting off made me throw the shirt onto the floor. I was embarrassed by how much I felt an attachment to Nicky. I couldn't let him know that. It would be much better if we didn't have any connection at all. After all the trouble I'd gotten him into, it would be best if once this was all over, we never saw each other again.

"Kasi, I just thought–" Nicky burst through the door with only a towel around his waist. He was way too tall for the small motel towels they provided anyway, but his size made it look like a napkin more than anything. I tried my best to focus on his face and not his chest glistening with water over his tattoos. "We should probably cut your hair while it's still wet. Might be easier."

"Yeah, sure. I'll be in in a second. Want me to bring the chair back?"

"Nah, we're good."

I waited just until I knew Nicky had slipped his boxers back on, then followed after him, trying to keep my hair off my neck.

"How short do you want it?" Nicky asked me, taking the entirety of my hair in one hand.

I winced. "Just go for it."

I closed my eyes, refusing to watch myself in the mirror. I didn't want to witness anymore of myself disappear. I already felt like such a different person than I had a few days ago. I couldn't see the final true parts of me fade as well.

"That's it."

I opened my eyes. I had expected it to take longer. I expected the sound of sawing, the pull against my scalp. But, there was nothing. All I saw when I looked around me was Nicky's hand, holding a good six inches of my hair.

"You look...nice." he whispered, regarding me in the mirror.

"I know I don't. You don't have to lie."

"I'm not lying, Kasi."

"I don't believe you, but thanks. You want some ice cream? I picked some up for us."

He paused, seemingly struggling with my self-evaluation and quick change in conversation. "Yeah, sounds good."

He grabbed a couple of spoons next to the coffee pot, handing me one as he sat down on the loveseat across from the bed. I fished the ice cream out of the Dollar General bag, looking at the flavor for the first time. Cookies and cream.

I sat down next to Nicky, opening the tub and offering him the first bite.

"Did you know this is my favorite?" he asked me, scooping out a large serving.

He slid the spoon over his lips, nearly swallowing the spoonful in one bite. I watched as his eyes fluttered close, his breathing softening. I tentatively took a bite myself, realizing the shock of the cold ice cream completely stunned me of breath myself.

We sat there together, eating scoops and scoops of ice cream until we'd nearly emptied the entire tub. Not once did either of us say anything. We just rested, in complete peace and silence for the first time in several days.

The feeling of clean clothes, fresh hair, a full stomach, and the absolute quiet made me drowsy with contentment. Of course, all that was in addition to Nicky's radiating benevolence. He didn't do anything. He just existed and I felt relief.

I turned my head just a touch to watch him out of the corner of my eye. He was sucking on his empty spoon, staring straight ahead of him into space. I couldn't help but smile and laugh a bit under my breath at the sight of him. He caught me then, his own face breaking into a grin.

"What?" he chuckled.

"Nothing." I whispered, hiding my mouth with my hand.

Nicky suddenly stood. "You like music, right?"

I nodded.

He moved across the room to the coffee bar where a small radio was perched on the closest end of the surface to us. With abrupt static, he turned it on, shifting the dials until he caught a coherent station. A soft song was playing, echoing into the silent room with an odd clarity as if the singer were truly singing to just us.

Nicky began to sway clumsily, holding up his hands as if he were a talented dancer and knew what he was doing. His beam hit me like a punching bag to the chest, knocking the air out of me with a whoosh of breath. I jumped up beside him, chuckling loudly, grabbing his hands to move them in a more methodical fashion.

"Like this." I mumbled, feeling him release the weight of his arms into my fingertips.

Once his arms had relaxed, I walked into him, moving his feet with my own. He followed unsteadily, shuffling himself against my own movements. We made a few turns around the room, our motions faster and faster as the song progressed. We laughed together as we tripped over our feet, finding we weren't nearly as talented with higher tempo.

With one grand movement, at the climax of the final chorus, Nicky spun me away from him, stretching our distance the length of our interlocked hands. As I rediscovered my ability to stand, I gasped, realizing how hard I'd been wheezing. Like mine, Nicky's chest rose and fell with heavy breaths, the top of his lip shining with sweat.

The effect of the song dwindled away as Nicky pulled me back into him, rolling me towards him like he was folding me in a blanket. When we met again, instead of grabbing my other hand, Nicky dropped the one he was holding, suddenly wrapping his arms around my shoulders, shoving his face into my neck.

"I'm so sorry, Kasi." he sobbed, hot tears beginning to fall down his cheeks onto my skin.

I slid my hands up his chest, pressing my palms into him as he held me, pulling me closer and closer. My lungs were restricted by the tightness of his embrace, but I mustered little pants despite it all. His bare chest against my ear was warm, his skin soft like a baby's.

"C'mere." I whispered, pushing myself away from him.

I couldn't bring myself to look into his face as I led him towards the bed, laying him into it. He continued to exhale messy sobs as I tucked him under the blankets, propping the pillows up under his head, tears burning my own eyes.

I knew despite everything I felt, I had to be strong in this moment. I couldn't let myself be the weak one. Seeing Nicky lie there as fragile as a child felt like a stab wound in my own gut. It hurt and burned and felt like fire. I ached immensely. I could hardly breathe. My lips, cold only moments ago from the ice cream, now trembled with warm cries waiting to be released.

I turned away, pressing my good hand to my mouth, holding everything I wanted to feel and say back.

"Kas." Nicky whimpered from behind me.

"Yeah?" I asked, my back still to him.

"Do you...wanna come cry with me?"

I nearly laughed. I nearly smiled. I nearly melted into a puddle at the foot of the bed, just waiting to be soaked up by the dirty motel room carpet.

But, I didn't.

Instead, I faced him and I climbed right into the bed beside him as he held the covers up for me. I wormed my way right into his arms, my sobs catching in my throat. Nicky pressed me into his chest, holding me, almost entirely enveloping me with his body. I could feel his wet lips and nose sink into my hair as he laid himself on my head. His sobs were more controlled than mine, but I could still feel him shaking with his grief.

It only took a second for me to release my own. And when I did, when we cried together, when we held each other, when we protected each other in that moment from everything and anything around us or coming for us or waiting for us, I felt truly real. As if I'd never been real before. It was a high like nothing had ever given me. I was disgusting, but I was real. We both were. Him and I.

Chapter 9

Exactly like a morning I'd had months ago, I woke to the bright
sun shining in through the curtains. Nicky laid behind me, wrapped
around me, his hands clutched to my abdomen. We were both damp
with sweat, my hair sticking to my neck with the moisture. The clock
on the bedside table read eleven-thirty, barely visible with its red digital
numbers outshined by the sun's rays. My stomach growled with
hunger the ice cream from last night had only minimally deterred.

I rolled over, throwing my arm around the back of Nicky's head.
His face was still sweet with sleep, but his eyelids had begun to shake as
I roused him. Carefully, I took a handful of his curls in my hand,
fluffing them and twisting them around my fingers. I was right in that
they'd bounce back, the wetness of our sweat soaked sheets surely
having contributed.

"Nicky?" I breathed, pressing my nose to his cheek.

"Mmm?" he mumbled, keeping his eyes closed.

"Do you want to go get something to eat?"

"Like food?"

"Yeah, like food."

"I like food."

"Me too."

He opened his eyes, squinting at me. "What time is it?"

"Food time."

"Okay. Um, but before that could I do something?"

"Yeah, what is it?"

Nicky sat up, stretching himself and rubbing the sleep from his eyes. "I wanted to write a letter to my sister. I don't know if I'll ever be able to get it to her, but I feel like I should."

"Alright. Here," I threw the blankets off my legs, wandering over to where the dirty beige phone in the room was. Beside it was a notepad and pen. I brought both back to Nicky, laying them on his lap. "You can use this. Take as much time as you need. I'll just be in the bathroom."

I left him with that and a half hour later we were dressed in new, fresh clothes, without a word between us about the letter. I knew how much his sister meant to him, and I wanted to respect his wish to not talk about it. I was positive it was difficult for him to possibly make promises to her he couldn't keep or wish her well in a future he might never have. I hated that I might have taken away that part of his life. I was afraid that my mistake had cost him his sister. If nothing else, the gesture was enough to secure my opinion of him in that he was as noble and as good as anyone could ever be. Thinking of someone else in as desperate a moment as this.

When we were ready, we stuffed our old clothes in the leftover plastic bags from the dollar store and Goodwill, shoving them under the bed before we left, our checkout time being later that afternoon since we'd gotten in so late. We figured we could clean up properly when we got back, but just wanted to make sure any housekeepers didn't find any incriminating evidence before we could.

There was a McDonald's we'd passed on our way to the motel only about ten minutes walking, so it was there we decided to stop for food. I got myself a hamburger, Sprite, and large fry, Nicky a Big Mac with Diet Coke and fries to go with it. We ate inside on the checkered tiled floor with our small little paper ketchup cups and napkins spread across the table.

We didn't talk about anything significant while we ate. Nothing about our situation. Nothing about the letter. We decided to just get to know each other. The simple things. What colors we each liked. What animals. Where we went to school or had wanted to go to school. Friends. Prior jobs. Hopes for the future.

It was hard to imagine a future where we got out of this. It was nice, though, to picture it for just a minute. To fully wash my memories of these past few days, cleansing every inch of myself of every bad thing that'd happened. My crimes. My pain. My inability to stay sober.

"I've always wanted to write music." Nicky told me, after taking a long drink of his Coke.

"Yeah?"

"I can actually play the piano pretty well. I don't think I'm the best singer, but I've written some lyrics before."

"What about?"

"Just about being lonely."

"Oh." I looked up at him, not knowing how to react.

"Nah, it's okay. I tend to pick the wrong people to get close to. I get lonely sometimes. That's boring, though. You don't wanna know about all that shit."

"I'm sorry."

"Don't be."

I desperately wanted to tell him that I hoped I wouldn't become one of those people he regretted getting close to. Truly, I felt like a fool to even entertain the idea that we were close or friends or had any real kind of connection. Besides that delusion I held on to, the idea of us ever continuing to get close was despicable. I was a monster. I had already sucked so much life out of him. I couldn't bear to do it anymore.

"I'd love to hear you play some time."

Nicky's face fell into a grin. "I'd love to play for you some time."

"Should we head out?"

"Alright, yeah."

After throwing out our wrappers and clearing our table, we headed back to the streets that had begun to busy with the lunch hour. Neither one of us was eager to go back to the motel, so we just ambled around, going up and down loud streets and looking into store windows. We eventually found a cute little park surrounded by trees in what felt like the city center. The trees reflected the season with artistic prestige. The red, orange, and yellow leaves littering the floor and dressing the trunks of the trees. It made the park seem like a completely remote place.

"Should we sit for a bit?" Nicky asked, pointing to a bench under a large maple.

I nodded, waiting for Nicky to lead the way, but, before he did, and most unexpectedly, he grabbed my hand. His touch startled me. I physically jumped a bit at the feeling, snatching my own hand back. I wasn't sure why it shocked me so much. Maybe it was purely an instinctive reaction to shy away from someone I'd already hurt so much.

"I'm sorry, I didn't mean to-"

"No...no," I interrupted. "I'm just cold." I lied, stuffing my hands into my jacket pockets.

To my relief, Nicky shrugged, shuffling his way through the leaves, crunching them with his sneakers. He cleared the leaves off the bench for me, letting me sit down first, then joined me. I wanted to sit as far away from him as I could, but there really was a brisk breeze and the idea of scooting closer to him was very tempting. I knew it would be better to practice restraint now, knowing soon there'd be a time when we'd never see each other again. It just made sense. We couldn't ever see each other again.

But, after all that we'd been through? All we'd experienced together. I didn't know what the right thing to do was.

As I sat there, sitting next to Nicky, watching him stare at the leaves, smelling the air, filling his lungs with cleanliness unlike we'd experienced lately, I had a gut-wrenching realization. There was something I could do. It was *the* thing to do. But, I didn't know if I could.

I remembered the feeling of holding him as he bawled, shaking with fear and anger and regret, and I realized I could make a choice. I had the power to turn myself in and save Nicky. All of this could be over. He could be safe. He could go home and write his music and be with his sister and forget about me.

It seemed almost too good to be true as I imagined him having his young adulthood back. It was everything that I wanted for him.

So, what was stopping me?

I was ashamed of how familiar the feeling was. It was the same thing that always stopped me. The same thing that made me crazy for all the unhealthiest things. I was scared out of my mind. I was so fucking scared.

I couldn't do it.

"Did you know I have a dog?" Nicky suddenly laughed, watching as a black labradoodle and its owner strode past us on the sidewalk.

"No, I didn't. What's its name?"

"His name is Milo. He's a little border collie. Bestest boy ever."

"I bet he is. I wish I had a dog."

"Have you ever had pets?"

"I had a cat once, but she was old and died when I was younger."

"Aww, I'm sure you miss her a lot."

I felt a smile spread across my face. "She was an orange cat. Dumb as fuck, but she was pretty cute. I loved her a lot. I was only six when she died, so I didn't really understand why my parents took her away and didn't bring her back. I kinda had shit parents. They never explained it to me, so I was just heartbroken."

"Kas-"

"Nope! Don't say you're sorry. I'm fine. They're not in my life anymore, anyway."

"Are they-?"

"Yeah, they're alive. I just don't really fit into their world. I'm not exactly welcome."

"Is it because of...like your drinking?"

My heart stopped, stomach twisted, face began to sweat, but before I could stop myself the truth fell out. "Yeah, actually. I've never told anyone this before, but it was a kind of intervention that started it. They told me that I would never see them again unless I quit. They said I was ruining my life and that I should be ashamed of the way I was handling myself. They told me I was hurting them and they couldn't bear to see me destroy everything they'd built for me."

"Kasi-"

"They weren't wrong," I stared straight into his face. "I *am* ruining my life. But, I don't care. Not about them. Not about the drinking. Not about my life. Not about living."

Nicky hesitated, his lips moving to form words, but none came.

"I know you think they were right." I said, putting my hands between my thighs to warm them.

"Kasi, I don't know your parents. I don't know why you do what you do. I don't know why you drink. I never knew why my dad drank. But, I never thought it was because he didn't care. I always thought he cared so much and hurt so deeply that he physically couldn't bear to exist in his reality anymore. He was hiding from his feelings, but never did he not care. He may not have cared very much for me, but he definitely had his reasons to drink and become numb to the responsibility of being a non-shitty father,

"I also find it hard to believe that you don't care. I've seen you care. I've seen you care a lot. About me, at least."

I caught his gaze again, my eyes watering without my consent.

"Look, I'm sorry for asking such an intrusive question. I care about you, Kasi. I want you to be okay, but more than that I want you to want to be okay. I *know* you care. I want you to care about yourself. I want good things for you."

"Why should you? After everything I did. After all the pain I've caused you?"

"All the pain you caused me? Kasi, we were attacked in the middle of the night by someone who didn't care about us at all. Who didn't care about anything at all. The hurt HE inflicted, yeah, that causes me some pain. That definitely fucked me up. But, that wasn't your fault. You didn't do that on purpose."

"But, I killed him," my voice broke to a whisper. "I killed him and I did what I always do when I'm scared and I ran. And I took you with me. I brought you with me and we've been running for days, terrified out of our minds because of a decision I made. That is something I did to cause you pain."

"You realize, at any point, I could've turned you in. That day when you cut your hand, I could've walked down the hall and spoken to the officers, gotten you arrested, and gone home."

"You should've done that. You should do that."

"Quite honestly, Kas, I've been acting on pure impulse ever since I walked into that god-forsaken Shell. I haven't been thinking about much of anything. Only, I saw what you did for me. I watched you save my life instead of abandoning me. Then, every day since then, I've seen you do everything you possibly could to keep me safe. You're not perfect at it, but you're struggling too. I can't imagine what you're feeling. It's because of all that, Kasi, that I haven't turned you in. Or turned myself in. I just have this pressing desire to make sure you're safe before I do anything else. I owe you my life."

"Nicky-"

"Shut up, idiot. I don't want to hear another word. I'm mad at you for bringing this up again. It wasn't your fault. I hate that you think that it was. We can't focus on what happened. We gotta keep our eyes ahead of us or we'll both crash."

"Nicky." I breathed, wrapping my arms around him.

I didn't deserve it. I didn't deserve him. But, he was right. My ability to care for myself was absolute garbage. My ability to care for him, though? Less garbage. At least, a little less garbage.

He rubbed my back, drawing me towards him so our legs touched. In contrast to the increasingly cooling air, he was like a warm fire, always bright and burning. I let myself relax under his embrace. I allowed myself, for just a second, to feel no regret or guilt by letting him comfort me. Being vulnerable was a very unfamiliar feeling, but it reminded me so greatly of how I'd felt last night. It wasn't a good feeling because on the inside I truly felt like shit and really only wanted something to drink, but it wasn't a feeling that brought on more pain. It merely stopped it from growing.

I hated that my brain immediately went to that dark place of needing something to drink. Needing something to burn my insides so bad that the emotional burn wouldn't hurt so much. I didn't want to have that desire. I couldn't stop it, though. Even Nicky couldn't stop it. It filled me with a kind of toxic rage. My heart could be repaired by pretty words, but my body? I needed something much stronger than that.

"I just thought," I started, sitting up to press my cold hands to my hot cheeks. Nicky looked into my eyes with tenderness, pushing my hair behind my ear. "What time do we have to check out of the motel?"

"Fuck. Probably right now."

I shook my head, pulling my jacket tighter around me.

"C'mon." Nicky groaned, standing up and holding his hand out for me.

This time I took it.

It was a rush to get back to our room and clear everything out; the day had really gotten away from us. Selfishly, I'd been hoping there would be one or two Corona cans left, waiting for me. It was the most pressing and motivating thing on my mind as we raced down sidewalks, trying to make it back before our things were dumped in the lobby. When we made it, we found we were just in time, and while Nicky gathered socks and underwear, I searched the room for any alcohol. It was to no avail, however, as the cleaning staff must have cleared it out. It was beyond likely there was a no alcohol policy here.

"Shit." I growled under my breath.

"We should take our old clothes with us." Nicky said aloud, shoving what looked like a bag of dirty clothes into my backpack.

"Good idea." I agreed, bending down to grab the final bag of my own clothes from under the bed.

"I guess they don't clean under the beds."

"Nope, sure don't."

"Our next place better have more thorough staff," he joked. "We most certainly cannot settle for such substandard cleaning practices. We have our health to think of."

"Exactly."

I reached my hands down in front of me, naturally, to stand, pushing my weight against my palms, but, as I did, a sharp, shooting pain shot up my arm with the injured hand.

"Fuck!"

"You alright?" Nicky's head appeared around the other side of the bed.

I turned my hand around and saw our makeshift bandage soaked through with blood. I had been so distracted by getting something toxic in my system I hadn't noticed how horribly it hurt. It ached a bit throughout the days and stung whenever anything pressed into it, but this was unlike anything I'd experienced apart from maybe the act of slicing it initially. I must have split the wound open when I pushed so hard against my hand, reversing any healing or scabbing that might've happened since the original injury.

"It's my hand." I whimpered.

"Oh, shit, Kas." Nicky knelt down at my side.

He took my arm in his hands and very gently started unwrapping the bandage. As it loosened, I could feel more blood pulsating at the base of my wrist, seeping steadily out of the opening. I almost couldn't stand to watch Nicky as he revealed my skin, but I wanted to know how much damage I'd caused as an almost sick punishment for not being more careful.

"Goodness, Kasi," Nicky mumbled, raising my hand so it was above my head. "Wait there a sec."

Awkwardly with my hand above me, I sat as he ran to the bathroom, grabbing a washcloth and soaking it with water. He brought it back dripping, squeezing it out over my hand and onto the floor. Most of the blood was flushed away with the water, but the wound was still actively bleeding. In addition to hot blood and exposed flesh, I could see a watery, yellowish-white liquid oozing from the deepest part of the cut. I wasn't a medical expert, but I knew what that meant.

"It's getting infected." I sighed, raising my hand back up.

"We have to get some real disinfectant for this. Not just vodka."

"We can't ask the hotel staff."

"No, of course not."

"What do we do then?"

I looked into Nicky's eyes and saw fearful distress in them. Even though I didn't exactly want to be, I was so destructively indifferent to the worsening of the wound, and I found I couldn't bring myself to care if it did get infected or not. But, seeing Nicky so worried made me realize my indifference was hurting him. I'd promised myself not to do that anymore.

I spoke quickly to fix it. "Hey, we could probably find a pharmacy around here. Let's just wrap it in a shitload of toilet paper, check out, and get some healing juice."

"Healing juice?"

"I don't know what it's called!"

Nicky chuckled roughly. "Fine."

He helped me stand, then we rinsed my hand under the sink, trying to wash out whatever we could. Even the light pressure of the water was miserable, but I bit my tongue to keep from groaning out. Afterwards, we wrapped my hand in almost an entire roll of toilet paper. It wasn't nearly as absorbent as what we'd put together before, but it would hold until we managed to get somewhere where we could find real bandages.

Nicky asked if I would wait outside the motel while he checked out to avoid the nosy eyes of the staff. I realized just how good of a decision that was while I waited for him, remembering the disappearing Corona. I'd already given them a reason to mark us as unstable. Seeing a botched bandage job on a profusely bleeding hand would certainly just make it ten times worse.

"Alright, let's go." Nicky told me quickly as he walked out.

He took my good arm as he met me, nearly dragging me down the street. I wasn't sure what had happened in there to make him so uneasy, but I trusted him. I let him guide me further and further along the sidewalk with my backpack on his back, looking straight ahead, not meeting my eyes for a second.

I hardly knew where we were anymore after ten minutes or so had passed. Nicky kept a stern, determined look on his face, which scared me a little. The pace he led us was not quite a run, but it was brisk enough to make a few heads turn as we went by. I tried to keep up as best as I could so it didn't seem as though I was being hauled away against my will, but it wasn't easy.

I finally had to say something. "Nicky, what's wrong?"

"You."

"Me? What did I do?" I gasped. "They didn't figure out who I was in there, did they? When you were checking out?"

He glanced down at me with his eyebrows furrowed. "Huh? No. No one recognized you. It's your hand. I'm really worried about it."

"Well, if that's all, can we slow down a little?"

"Oh, yeah." Nicky quieted his pace, releasing his grip on my arm a bit.

As we stopped our sprint-walking and my adrenaline slowed, I found the pain in my palm returning. I balled my fingers together, trying to stem the stabbing that was rising up my forearm, but I only stretched the cut further by making such a motion. I yelped out, raising my hand to my chest as blood began to spill more like water down my wrist.

"Here. This will work." Nicky stopped walking, pivoting us into the parking lot of a Walgreens.

Hesitating only for a red suburban to pass, we nearly jogged our way inside; Nicky ahead of me, not waiting long enough for the automatic doors to fully open.

"Take your arm out of your sleeve." he whispered, grabbing a basket off the stack beside the shopping carts.

"What?"

"Hold on."

Nicky set down the basket and pulled my good hand and arm out of my jacket sleeve. He gently slid it back over my shoulder, drawing my bloodied hand across my chest onto my right side. With clumsy, but fast fingers, he pulled the other side of my jacket farther over my shoulder, so my arm was covered at least past my wrist.

"Keep it there, okay?"

I nodded, following him as he strode away frantically, his head on a swivel. I kept my eyes on the shelves too, looking for anything I thought could be of use to us. Nicky had success before I did, finding and taking a few bottles of saline wound solution off a shelf. Beside it, I recognized bacitracin ointment and grabbed it, tossing it into the basket with the saline. Down the next aisle, we found packets of gauze and bandage wrap. We made sure to get several packages of both of those, agreeing that we needed to be changing my bandage more often.

It only took us a few minutes to gather everything, but in that short time, the bleeding had only worsened, the smell becoming very obvious to more than just myself. The hot, gushing liquid had completely soaked the toilet paper now and was beginning to stain the shirt that I held it against. The metallic scent filling my nose as well as the bright fluorescents and the quick pace of Nicky made me dizzy, my feet moving separately to the rest of my body.

"Nicky, I don't feel good." I groaned, leaning up against a shelf at the end of one of the aisles.

"Oh, fuck, Kasi." He dropped the painkillers he'd been holding to the floor, rushing over to clutch my shoulder. "Look at me. Look at my eyes."

I stared straight at him, my vision beginning to go blurry.

"Alright, that's it. C'mon."

He steered me back towards the front of the store, throwing the full basket onto the counter by the register. The man working there wore a pharmacist's coat and was restocking the shelf behind him with packets of cigarettes. His hands still held three boxes when he turned to us, answering the eager grunt of Nicky.

"Can I help you?" he asked, his face severe.

"We're ready to check out."

"I'm in the middle of something at the moment, could you wait just a second?"

"NO!"

The man raised his eyebrows, clearly affronted at being talked back to.

"Listen," Nicky panted, shoving the basket closer to the pharmacist across the counter. "We'll buy whatever you're holding so you don't have to shelve it, okay?"

"These?" he offered, holding up the cigarettes.

"Yeah, they're fine. We're really in a hurry."

The pharmacist rolled his eyes, setting the packets of cigs down on the counter, punching his fingers unhurriedly into the register. He gazed at me for a fraction of a second as he began ringing things up and stopped short.

"Are you feeling okay, miss?" he asked me.

"I'm fine." I breathed, realizing just how airy my voice was starting to sound.

"You look really pale."

"I have the flu." I spat, unintentionally flinging saliva out of my mouth.

I didn't plan on trying anything to expedite the checking out process, but my lie worked. The man clearly didn't want to make me stand here any longer than he had to, so his hands moved in double time, working just about as fast as Nicky's foot was tapping against the floor. In under a minute, he had all our things bagged, our cash stored in the register, and our receipt in Nicky's hand. His last words of "have a nice day" were barely out of his mouth by the time we'd gone back through the squeaky sliding doors and into the parking lot.

With our bag in hand, we crossed the street to an abandoned gas station, hiding around the side away from the traffic. Nicky immediately tore open the plastic bag, reaching his hand in for something specific. I was slightly surprised to find him pull out one of the packs of cigarettes and hand one to me. He then took a lighter out of his wallet, lighting the end of the cig in my mouth.

"Sit down, Kasi, can you lean against here?" he urged me, helping me down onto my butt.

The cool brick on the side of the building reminded me that there did still exist consistent temperature. On the walk out of the Walgreens, my head had begun to sweat, my neck and torso growing cold. I tried to focus on the cigarette between my lips. The stale flavor, the warm smoke, the soft, mucusy paper. It was all I could do not to shout out in pain. Although, I was quickly losing the energy to manage even that.

Even with the fogginess in my mind, I was able to unwrap my hand as Nicky opened everything on top of the bag, setting down an opened packet of gauze, the bacitracin ointment with the lid unscrewed, and a bandage roll with a small piece of it unfolded from the rest. Once I'd gotten the sopping wet toilet paper off my palm, Nicky took my wrist in his hand, spilling one bottle of the saline solution from the tips of my fingers all the way down to the base of my hand.

I screamed. Pure agony just echoing from my lungs, shaking my entire body. My cigarette fell from my mouth to the ground beside me, landing in a nasty bit of gravel. I knew it was hopeless to try to grab it again, for I could not stop the pain escaping my throat. With my free hand, I instead cupped my mouth, trying to force myself to quiet down as I began to weep.

Through my tears, I could see Nicky bending over me still, pouring more and more solution until he'd cleaned my hand enough to put anything else on it. I blinked, focusing on his face, staring at his beautiful nose and cheeks and eyes. There were tears in his too, but they fell more gracefully down his face unlike mine.

He shook my hand, hoping to rid it of any extra moisture, eventually blowing on it with his hot breath. Once satisfied, he took the bacitracin ointment tube, squirting a large glob onto a piece of gauze. It seemed almost half the bottle was emptied by the time he was done, finally smoothing it around with his hand for even coverage. He blew on my palm one last time before picking up and carefully placing the gauze facedown on my hand. With a cringe moving across his own face, he pressed down on top of the gauze, forming it and the ointment to the shape of my hand. I sucked on my tongue, begging myself to withhold another scream.

"I'm almost done." Nicky moaned, reaching with both hands for the bandage.

He started at the back of my hand, holding the bandage steady against my skin, then slowly began wrapping it around, up and over my palm, around my thumb, and all the way down across my wrist. I hardly paid attention to the number of wraps, but I knew as soon as he was finished, there was no chance any major bleeding would leak through it. I didn't feel immediately better, but I knew we'd stopped the bulk of my blood loss, which had to be good.

As he finished, Nicky rocked back onto his heels, shoving his face into his shirt. I placed my injured hand back across my chest, reaching out my right hand to grab Nicky's shoulder. He looked up at me as I touched him, his face red and distorted with pain.

"Thank you." I sobbed, leaning my head back against the brick.

Unexpectedly, he seized my hand from his shoulder, bringing it around towards him so he could kiss my palm, salty with my tears. He then placed his nose against it, inhaling deeply and exhaling with strength.

Chapter 10

We sat still for a long time, both of us just catching our breath. The more I rested, the better I felt, feeling my power return with every second. Nicky kept my good hand in his, holding it, tracing my palm lines with his finger, rubbing my knuckles and fingers individually. It was a repetitive action, never straying from the slow rhythm. It kept that part of me warm at least. I wasn't as freezing as I'd been before, the sweat on my forehead having almost completely disappeared. However, the later it got into the afternoon and evening, the colder the concrete below us would become. The colder we would become.

"Nicky?" I finally asked him, taking my hand away.

"Mmm?"

"Do you want to get some dinner? Get off the street and somewhere warm?"

He nodded. "Yeah, good idea."

He leaned forward, gathering our assortment of items back into the bag, pocketing the opened cigarette pack. I tried to stand on my own, but it was hard with only one functioning hand. I could move the injured one, but it was extremely tender and putting any extra weight on it would be a mistake. I compromised by pushing myself backwards into the brick wall, using my feet to help shuffle myself upright.

"Hey, hey, take a minute. Are you feeling alright? Dizzy?" Nicky hissed at me, reaching out to steady me.

I brushed him off. "I'm fine. I swear."

I wasn't exactly fine.

My legs felt tingly, my vision was cloudy, the pain in my hand unbearable, and I felt so nauseous that I could've thrown up on the spot if I inclined my head forward and down even the slightest bit. This was information, though, that I wouldn't dare share with Nicky. I'd ruined the day. I could protect him from at least this.

"If you're ready, we should start walking." he told me, his head moving left to right, searching our surroundings.

I moved without him, hobbling my way back around the gas station and towards the road where more cars had started to congregate, most with their headlights on, the rush hour beginning. Nicky caught up to me, insisting that I take his arm for balance. I didn't argue with him, truly unsure of how far I could make it on my own.

Surprisingly, it seemed moving was helping. The more we walked, the more energy I felt. It could very well be the adrenaline hiding the pain in my arm or the blood finally flowing to the correct parts of my body, but whatever it was, it was making every movement easier. I found I could do more than just look at the ground in front of me, focusing intensely on my every step. I could actually look around me, ahead and behind, scanning what was around us, trying to find somewhere to eat. It was a good feeling to be helpful.

And helpful I was. I was the one who found the cozy little Mexican restaurant at the top of a hill just starting to take customers for dinnertime. I was determined to treat us. After all Nicky had done and paid for for me, I was more than overdue to pay him back. I knew by this point, most of our funds were limited. At least, the cash was, but I figured I had enough to pay for a decent dinner at least, maybe even a night at a hotel too.

We got a table at the back of the restaurant, and I ordered myself a large chicken quesadilla; Nicky chimichangas. We shared a bowl of salsa between us, not worrying ourselves with double-dipping at this point. I could tell Nicky watched me the whole time, his eyes pinned on me and my hand, laying across the table. I met his eyes occasionally, but every time I did, he pounded me with questions.

"How many times do I have to tell you?" I grumbled at him. "I'm okay."

Again, that was a lie. I was better than I had been thirty minutes ago, but now that the initial agony had subsided, the consistent, aching pain put one thought and one thought only into my brain. I needed a fucking drink.

I hadn't had anything in so long. It was making me crazy. I could feel my core beginning to shake, my muscles tensing, my head pounding. I knew this feeling better than anything. I knew how bad it could get. My parents had tried brutally forcing me to quit before and the withdrawal I experienced made me lose my mind. I was having hallucinations, panic attacks, intense body aches so bad I could barely move except to scream. I couldn't be near that level now as it had been only twenty four hours or so, but if I didn't get something strong soon to ease all of this pain (inside and out), I might quit literally combust.

"You'll tell me if you're not okay, right?" Nicky asked, his eyes seemingly penetrating right through me.

"Yes, mom." I laughed, taking my hand off the table, hiding it in my lap.

As the evening went on and as more and more people started filing into the restaurant, we realized we'd need to leave to find another hotel sooner rather than later. If we timed it wrong, we'd get to a hotel as a lot of people were checking in for the night, and it was a bad idea for us to be in busy places for long. The more brief our interactions with other people were the better.

Nicky argued with me over the bill, but I paid it in full, telling him he could pay for the hotel instead. Although, I did still fully intend to pay for that myself too. He had done too much for me today for it to be otherwise.

When we left through the glass front doors and stepped back out into the evening, both of us shivered, pulling our jackets tighter around us. An uncomfortable wind had picked up since we'd gone inside, whirling around us and pushing us down onto the sidewalk. Anyone walking by would have trouble recognizing us given our hoods were pulled up tight, our hands and faces buried in our coats.

We huddled together, jogging our way down the street, not quite knowing where we were going. We'd had luck before just wandering around aimlessly until we found what we were looking for, so the decision to continue that pattern was made without any communication at all. Both of us just knew to keep walking. Anywhere and everywhere until something worked.

Ahead of us down the street I could see lights flashing through the windows of a building, lighting up the sidewalk and road. As we got closer, I could hear music playing, the bass reverberating against the shop walls beside it. Even from a distance, I could smell the heat of the inside, and probably more importantly, I could smell the alcohol.

When we approached the brick exterior, I stopped us to get a better look inside. It was obvious this place was intended for the warmer weather. There was a glass garage door blocking most of the front of the building, most likely intended to be open during the day with bar height round tables scattered half in half out. Because of the weather, I could see everything pushed inside through the glass;

outdoor chairs stacked together out of the way of the more permanent booths and long tables. It looked like some kind of bar and grill, but it seemed tonight was special since most of the customers were not sitting and eating but were instead standing congregated around a stage at the back of the room.

A couple walked out beside us, laughing and joking as they bundled themselves up in their coats. As the door opened, I could hear the music beyond just a rumble, flowing out like a wisp of smoke in the street. I knew immediately what was going on. They had a live band.

"Nicky, do you wanna go in for a sec?" I asked, gazing up into his eyes that were trained on me in that same concerned, protective way they had been earlier.

"Are you feeling good enough? I really think we should find somewhere for you to rest."

"Nicky, listen." I grabbed his arm, moving around him so we were standing face to face.

I prepared myself to beg. I prepared myself to appear pitiful and dejected. I prepared myself to be desperate. Then, I realized what I was doing. I was preparing myself to manipulate him into taking me in there so I could get something to drink. I was disgusted at the notion, but not long after my recognition of myself, a wave of insane alcohol lust rushed through me as it always did when I got close to breaking free of its hold. The memory of liquid fire sloshing down my throat made my tongue prickle, my lips dry. I was a vampire to it. My conscience played no part in this. Not even the guilt I felt for hurting Nicky could stop me.

I hated it. But, I couldn't ever get enough.

"I need a drink," I began, piecing my story together in my mind, finding the best way to break him. "My hand is killing me. It'll just take the edge off. I need something. Please."

His stare was long and hard. Ice cold, even. "You're an adult, Kasi," I could sense despondency in his voice. "I can't tell you want to do."

"Yeah, right."

"And, I'm an adult, too, which means I have to be honest with you. First, I was the one that took the Corona out of the motel room earlier. It was selfish. But, I thought I finally saw the real you and I wanted to keep her. It was almost instinctual that I did it. I did that for my dad too when I was younger. It never stopped him."

"I-"

"I'm not finished," there was anger in his eyes. "Second, I know I can't stop you from doing it, but please let me help you find another way. We can get pain meds somewhere if your hand is truly that bad or go to a doctor-"

"Nicky, we can't fucking do that!"

"Don't yell at me."

"Look, I'm sorry. I just...I just need it."

"Yeah," his face dropped, his shoulders drooping. "I know."

I was so conflicted. For years, I'd neglected myself. I hadn't cared whether I lived or died, but suddenly, me not being okay was hurting someone. It was different than with my parents. It was more than just responsibility for him. At least, I wanted to think so. I wanted so badly to make Nicky not hurt anymore. But, helping Nicky meant that I had to help myself. I had to find it within me to stop. I just couldn't do that. I knew it in my heart. I wasn't strong enough to care. Not about myself. Not yet.

I spun away from him, barging inside. I strode directly up to the
bar, squeezing between people dancing and singing along to the band.
A young woman stood, working behind the bar, fresh drink glasses in
her hand. She saw me coming, a bit of a quizzical look in her eye at my
appearance, but she didn't stop what she was doing. With an air of
nonchalance and patience, she put her glasses down, wiped her hands
on her apron, then approached me.

"What can I get you, hun?"

"Can I have a sex on the beach, please?"

"That'll be five."

I reached around me for my backpack that I wasn't wearing. I
even used my bad hand, forgetting the pain for a moment in my
eagerness. The tearing I could feel in my flesh snapped me back to
reality long enough for me to let out a small squeak of agony.

A hand unexpectedly grabbed my shoulder. "Here."

It was Nicky. He handed me a five dollar bill, then turned and
walked away towards the back of the room. I stood there, watching
him, speechless for a second. His gracefulness and purity made my
stomach twist with shame. A shame so heavy I felt I could almost
collapse. And yet, my go to for feeling such pain had been and always
was to go for a drink. Make the pain worse in other ways, so I never
had to feel the real stuff. I could feel both desires pulling at me so
immensely. I knew I could make a choice and end everything. Well,
end it for one person. Whatever I chose, I could end suffering for
someone.

"Miss?" the bartender tapped her knuckles on the wooden bartop.

A woosh of pain nearly buckled my knees. My decision was made.
I wasn't strong enough.

I handed her the money, then moved out of the way. I was tempted to turn around and catch Nicky's eye, but I knew how much it would hurt me if I did. I hated myself more than I ever had in my whole life for traumatizing him in this way. I never wanted to put him in that position. I never wanted my "problem" to trigger him with his past. I never expected to meet someone who made me want to be different so badly.

The all too familiar sound of a cold, condensation covered glass hitting the wooden surface and sliding towards me thrust my thoughts in another direction. Before the bartender could lift her fingertips from the edge of the cup, I had taken it within my own, swallowing half of it in one go. It wasn't as strong as what I was used to, but I could feel the slight tingly, burning sensation in my throat beginning to distract me from my feelings.

Loud clapping sounded from all around me, making me jump. The band had just finished a song and people were starting to disperse back to tables and seats at the bar. I saw a group of three guys and a girl coming towards me, maybe a little older than I was. They didn't notice me at first, sitting down beside me, ordering more drinks. I could tell the guys were a bit loopy already, the one furthest away from me singing to himself as he rocked on his chair.

After he ordered, the shortest of the men turned to me, a wide smile on his face. "It's Monroe! It's Marilyn Monroe!"

I'd almost forgotten my startling white blonde hair. I probably did look a bit like Marilyn Monroe. I was disgustingly unlike her, though. It was almost monstrous to compare me to her. She had been beautiful and wonderful and loved. I couldn't bring myself to believe I was any of those things.

"Fuck! It is! Damn, Monroe." his singing buddy chimed in.

"Let's buy her another drink. Whatcha want, Monroe." the first guy asked me.

A growing anxiety had begun to swell in the pit of my stomach, but I was being made an offer I couldn't refuse. "I'd do some shots with you."

They all ooo-ed at the challenge, wasting no time in buying us a set of shots. People around us noticed what we were up to and gathered for a show. I knew I would blow these idiots out of the water with my ability to down straight alcohol, but I kept it slow at first. I really only cared about the free drinks.

It was like breathing for me. As natural as an inhale and an exhale. I took one, then another, then another, then another.

I lost count by the time I realized I was standing on the bar, my hair soaked with sweat, my blood pounding in my ears, and my hand holding a bottle of wine. There was a crowd of people below me, repeating lyrics I hardly knew at all. I shook my head around, dancing with my whole body, kicking my feet out, flailing my arms. Some wine spilled from the bottle in my hand, drenching my arm down to my elbow.

"Shit! This is too expensive to be spilling!" I shouted, lowering myself down onto my bottom, dangling my feet over the edge of the bar.

One of the guys from before came up to me, taking hold of my ankles with his hands. He eyed me, naughtily, then reached his head towards my arm. I wasn't sure what he was doing at first, but then I felt his wet, spongy tongue glide up my arm. As he began to suck the wine with his lips from my skin, his hands rose gradually and greedily up to my knees, then to my thighs.

I screamed.

With as much force as I could muster, I brought my knees up to my chest, then slammed my feet down with an almighty kick into the guy's chest. He toppled backwards into the crowd, falling into people with their backs turned to him. The girl who had been with the group earlier narrowed her eyes at me, yelling loudly. Over the screeching music and my heart hammering in my chest, I couldn't hear a word she said. I could only assume the worst.

And she did, in fact, mean the worst. In a flash, she stomped over to me and slapped me hard across the face. She then grabbed my hair in her other hand, kneeing me in the stomach. I doubled over from the pain, but she caught me in the nose with a punch. I could feel myself start to bleed, a hot wetness trickling down onto my top lip.

"What'd you do that for, cunt!" she hollered, using my hair to pull our faces closer together.

"Your boyfriend fucking groped me?!"

"Stop acting like a whore if you don't want that to happen to you! You're a freak! Who the fuck even are you?"

I couldn't remember my name. I couldn't remember where I was or who I was supposed to be with. I could sense a distant feeling of guilt, but I pushed it away with every last bit of frailty I had.

"Monroe?" I breathed, my eyes clouding over.

"Yeah, my ass." the girl tossed me away in a huff, spinning around to the guy on the ground who was clutching his chest and gasping.

I lifted a hand up to my nose, trying to wipe the blood away. But, it was coming too fast for a wipe to send it off. I moved back around to the bar, hoping to grab some napkins when a sudden scream made me whip back around. The girl had come back for round two and was holding a beer bottle over her head with the intention of hitting mine with it. She was only a foot away by the time I faced her, so I had little time to accept my fate.

That was when the most surprising thing happened. A tall man with dark curly hair and tattoos on his neck stepped between us, catching the wrist of the girl with the bottle. He squeezed her hand fiercely, shaking her whole arm with his effort.

"Let go!" he snarled.

She whimpered, then dropped the bottle. It crashed onto the floor, breaking into thousands of shards that went flying all around us. Within seconds, the music died and the regular lights came back on, the flashing strobes turned off. A weak voice shouted firm words, signaling a time to leave.

The man who had saved me let go of the woman, turning around and locking eyes with me after she'd backed away. I realized instantly who it was.

"Nicky." I cried, bringing my arm up to cover my eyes so he couldn't see them.

I was so embarrassed. It was all slowly coming back to me. Beyond humiliating myself, I'd put Nicky in danger again. I'd done the worst possible thing I could've done to him. I'd hurt myself.

Soft, gentle hands pried my own away from my face. "I stepped outside for a second to get some air, Kasi. I'm so sorry."

"You? You are sorry?"

"What? C'mon we need to get out of here. I can't hear you."

I gladly set the wine bottle down on the counter, shuffling my way towards the door. The cold night air was like a blast to my sweaty skin, but it felt nice. It had begun to rain, thunder rumbling distantly, and icy droplets pelted me in the face as we left the cover of the building. The brisk nip of pain felt good. I felt like I desperately deserved it.

Nicky was behind me in a second, taking me by my good arm and helping me to walk down the street. I held onto him like a lifeline, clinging to every last bit of comfort before I did the unthinkable. I knew now that I'd been wrong to suffer such a moment of weakness. The first opportunity I had, I had to flag down someone and turn myself in. I had to end this. For Nicky. This was too much.

The sidewalk was wiggling, the ground below me moving almost like a conveyor belt taking me along with it. I tried to stand steady, but it was hard. I focused so intently on my leg movements. One after the other after the other. I tried to take deep breaths, flushing the toxins from my mind. I begged myself to think clearly. I needed to apologize to Nicky before I did anything.

"Nicky-" I started, but I couldn't get a word out.

Nicky didn't say anything. He only continued walking, the rhythm of his movements always the same. Always steady.

I tried again. "I'm so-"

I couldn't do it.

A stoplight ahead of us turned green and a dozen cars with bright headlights began barreling up the hill towards us, blurred only a little by the increasing rain. I closed my eyes to avoid the light, but it made it so much more difficult to continue moving. Closing my eyes only made everything swirl, my brain spinning on its axis, my body beginning to go with it. I could almost feel myself leaning into the traffic, being hit by a car and ending all this suffering.

Before I could fall, however, Nicky caught me. As he always did. He grabbed me with purpose, hoisting me up into his arms. I opened my eyes, throwing my forearms around his neck in a panic. I clung to him, shielding my face away from the headlights, burrowing my nose into his neck. I expected warmth, but I didn't expect to find complete dampness. His shirt was wet with both frozen rain and tears still streaming down his cheeks.

I wanted to die at the sight of him. I wanted the infection in my hand to grow, poisoning my blood, killing me in that second. He deserved so much more than this.

It took immense courage, but I swallowed hard and told him what I'd been wanting to since the day I met him. "I'm so tired of this, Nicky. I'm tired of you catching me when I fall and saving me. It's not fair. I feel helpless and like a child. I should be strong. I should be able to resist. I ruined everything. I'm so, so sorry."

I could hardly breathe by the time I finished the last word. Nicky's face fell as I spoke, his lip quivering, his eyes still gushing.

"You don't understand. I'm not mad, Kasi. What I saw tonight was someone in pain. Pain that I can't fix. It's killing me. You're killing yourself, Kas, and I can't fix it. I couldn't fix it for my dad. I can't fix it for you. I don't know what to do."

"I know. I know. I can't keep doing this to you. I'm turning myself in the first chance I get."

"What!" he stopped walking, staring straight into my face. "Don't you dare say that. Don't you fucking say that."

"But, why! Why not! It's what I should've done all along. I have to."

"Kasi, you don't understand! If you hadn't ki-done what you did, I'd probably be dead. If you didn't risk everything to save me, we wouldn't be here. You can't throw all that away now."

"Nicky, I wanted to run. I didn't want to save you. I was scared. I didn't want to die."

"But, you did anyway!"

"I don't even know why! You're no one to me!"

"Do you mean that?"

I hesitated. I had a choice to be honest. After everything that happened tonight, I couldn't afford to lie anymore.

With a sigh, I closed my eyes, not wanting to see his reaction. "No. Not at all. But, I have to think like that. I can't keep putting you in danger. If I distance myself from you now, I might actually save you for real. What this is right now is not what being saved should look like. Neither of us are free. This isn't happiness. Your association with me has ruined your life. I'm going to save you, Nicky, if it's the last thing I ever do. I really really care a lot about you, Nicky. For so many selfish reasons. I'm saving you. That's final."

"And what about you?"

"I'm not worth being saved."

"I think you're wrong."

I peered at him, loosening my grip on his neck just a little. "You've been so good to me. Every single minute since we met. You've taken care of me in every possible way. I have to take care of you for once."

"You really wanna take care of me, Kasi?"

"I do."

"Then shut up and pay for this stupid hotel."

We'd stopped in front of the entrance to a small parking lot with stone signs perched in small gardens on either side, repeating the hard to pronounce title of the hotel. It was a tall multistory building that rose high above us into the windy, thunderous city sky. Some of the windows glowed yellow, others were as black as the night. There were a decent amount of cars in the lot, not an unusual amount but not too few either. It seemed perfect.

I didn't dare say a word and let Nicky move us across the pavement towards the porte-cochère that shone in contrast to the blackness of the parking lot. He set me down before we got in sight of the sliding glass doors, being very careful not to touch my hand or bleeding face. With his enthralling gentility, he helped me to balance myself, then took my hand as we walked inside together to book a room.

Chapter 11

The lobby was empty. The tile floor squeaked as we walked over it, our feet slippery from the rain. Distant thunder became clearer and a few lightning flashes flickered through the sliding doors we'd just walked through. The receptionist's eyes were on us immediately, her face beaming with a faux white smile. At the sight of her perfection, I became self-conscious of my bleeding nose.

There were a few couches and coffee tables in the center of the open room, all either dark oak wood or deep black leather. I noticed a box of tissues on the coffee table closest to me and jogged over to it, stuffing a few in my face. The stench of the blood was becoming more noticeable to me the less toxins I flooded my body with. The absence of the alcohol was already feeling unbearable, but I knew I had things to do first. Nicky needed taken care of.

"So sorry, ma'am." I said, confidently, taking my backpack from Nicky's back and plunging my hand inside for my wallet.

"*I* am sorry. Is there anything we can get you for your bloody nose? A cold compress, perhaps?" she asked, contorting her face from welcoming to courteous concern.

"No, I am fine. Terrible allergies, right?"

"This rain should settle things, I hope."

"Yes, me too. Anyway, we'd like just one night please, and I was hoping to pay now?"

"Of course. Will that be two beds or just one?"

I turned to Nicky, not knowing if he'd want to share a bed with me after all I'd done to him today. I certainly wouldn't if I was him.

"The one will be fine." he nodded at her, running his hand through his dripping hair.

"Alright, that'll be $120 for the night."

I was glad I often kept large sums of cash in my wallet for when I needed to buy alcohol. When I was living with my parents, they had access to my bank account and would track my card and purchases. They had no ability to cut me off because the account was my own, but seeing my excess purchasing of alcohol began the hounding that ruined our relationship. Ever since then, I carried cash with me at all times to hide it from them. I never thought I'd be using it one day to hide from the police for a murder I committed.

I handed the lady the cash, making sure to keep my bad hand out of sight as much as possible. In return, she handed us a keycard, then directed us to the elevators. We both moved towards them in silence while I tried desperately to breathe through my mouth so I didn't have to smell the blood. I was becoming dizzier by the second, my stomach churning everything I'd eaten and drank today. The jerking and abrupt rising of the elevator did nothing to help.

By the time we stepped out into the hall, I knew I had only a little time before I started getting sick. I selfishly took Nicky's hand, closing my eyes and letting him guide me towards the room. We were on a high floor so it took much longer than I'd hoped to make it all the way up there. Even though I knew it was untrue, the height made my brain envision the building swaying and shifting with the wind. Every rumble of thunder only made that feel more real, sending jolts of anxiety bouncing through me in addition to nausea.

Although I did not see it, I heard the swiping of the card in the door, then the click and shove of the door falling open. I squinted my eyes for a brief second to spot a trash can beside the tv stand with a small gray bag inside it. I lunged in its direction, grabbing it just in time. Everything that was inside me came out then in a near-projectile vomit, spewing from both my mouth and my nose. The fluid that dribbled from my nose burned with the stomach acid, but also with the metallic blood scent.

"Fuck!" I moaned, dropping to my knees.

Nicky's arms suddenly wrapped around me, pulling me to a couch across the room. He set me up in it as I began hurling again, then sat beside me, a box of tissues in his hand. Without asking, he took one from the box and began wiping my lips, nose, and cheeks. Every gross inch. It was fruitless because the second he wiped me clean I began throwing up again, but he never stopped trying. With one hand he cleaned me, with the other he rubbed my back. He even started humming, trying to soothe in whatever way he could.

It felt like forever before the bulk of the vomiting stopped, but after what was more like fifteen minutes, I could breathe clearly again, my mouth dry, my throat on fire. A few tears trickled down my face as I sat up from the trash can in my hands, my eyes watering from the effort of the retching.

"Do you think you're done?" Nicky whispered, holding his hands out for the bin.

"For now, yeah," I sighed, clutching it further into my chest. "I'm not letting you take this. That's so disgusting."

"Kasi, I don't fucking care. Give it to me."

He wrenched the trash can out of my hands and took it to the bathroom. I heard him dump most of the puke in the toilet, flush it, then crumple up the bag and throw it somewhere else. He brought the bin back out to me, setting it down in front of me with a fresh trash bag inside.

"Thank you, Nicky."

"Of course."

He sat back down next to me, taking my shoulders and laying me down in his lap. I wasn't expecting him to do this, but unclenching and relaxing my exhausted body was exactly what I needed. The pounding in my head slowly quieted to only a soft ache, my heart rate reduced from its place of high adrenaline, and my skin began to cool from the hotness of exertion. Nicky brushed his fingers through my hair, sometimes gliding them across my skin. His touch was pacifying. It made the whirlwind in my brain settle. Even if it was only for now.

"Did you know what I was doing the day we met?"

He started speaking without warning, his voice soft but thoughtful. I turned myself to face him and saw his eyes were off in the distance.

"No, I have no idea."

"I think I was about to crash my car and die."

I sat up so fast I almost fell off the couch. I brought both my legs up onto the cushion, shifting myself so I was facing Nicky entirely.

"What?"

He smiled absently and looked at me. "Not intentionally. Accidentally."

"That's awful."

"It was a pretty horrible day. That morning I found out all my friends had ditched me to go to a concert for my favorite band. They knew how much I loved them, but for some reason they left me out. I know that's such a childish reason to be upset, but it put me in such a bad mood for the rest of the day."

"Well, of course it did. Anyone would be hurt by that. I'm so sorry."

"I had no idea just how terrible the day would become. I was moping, right, sad about my shitty friends. I mouthed off to my step-dad, not realizing what it would do, and my mom kicked me out of the house. I'm not even kidding. She banned me from ever going back there or speaking to my sister or trying to contact any of them. She said that they'd had enough of me. I was too much for them and I had to go."

I took his hand, not knowing what to say. As I wrapped myself around him, he stared at our intertwined fingers, thinking.

"I fought with her. I think I thought she loved me enough to think about what she was telling me. It was so out of the blue. At least for me it was. I have a feeling it was premeditated, and they were just waiting for me to make a mistake that justified what they were going to do. I was worried for my sister more than anything. My step-dad's a dick. I have no idea what he'd do to her without me there to take all his verbal abuse. He didn't like that I had something to say about my mom's decision, which I think was really his all along. He sucker punched me in the gut, then threatened to hurt me further if I didn't get out right then,

"So, I got in my car and drove. I started crying after a few minutes, becoming hysterical really quickly. I got on the highway without thinking and began speeding way beyond what any sane person would drive. I remember swerving in and out of cars, falling out of the lane onto the berm, nearly hitting the guardrails in places,

"I think that day just set me off. Years of neglecting to deal with my fucked up head had finally come crashing down. Years of abuse from both my dads. Indifference about everything from my mom. Feeling such loneliness even when my friends weren't assholes. Feeling an overwhelming need to protect my sister from every harmful thing I'd had to experience. All of that just collapsed onto me in that moment,

"Then, something kind of crazy happened. It's the reason, Kasi, why I followed you out of the Shell that night. I saw the lights of the gas station coming up ahead, and I just felt a strong sense of urgency to stop. I had no idea why. I just knew I had to stop and go inside. The minute I saw you, I understood why. I didn't know you from anywhere, but the instant I saw you, I knew we needed each other. I know it sounds stupid, but-"

"It doesn't sound stupid." I leaned into him, crushing him in a hug.

He wrapped his arms back around me, burying his face in my hair.

"Nicky, you are so strong. It's amazing how wonderful of a person you turned out to be despite how many horrific things you've had to go through, including this. I wish I was half as strong as you. You are so kind and sensitive. I can't even begin to thank you for everything you've done for me even though I know I don't deserve it. This world is lucky to have you. You are such a precious, innocent gift. You're purity in its most concrete form. But, you're also human and it's remarkable just how much courage you have to cry. To let yourself be weak. It makes me want to be a better person. YOU make me want to be a better person."

I sat away from him, taking his face in my hands. I brushed his eyebrows with my thumbs, staring into his beautiful dark eyes. His hands moved to my waist, bringing me closer to him. As he always did, he radiated warmth. It was hard not to completely melt under his gaze. It was like a net, constantly swooping towards me to keep me there. I grinned widely without realizing, the muscles in my face relaxing.

Nicky sighed. "I feel so safe with you. I think I trust you more than I trust anyone else in the world."

"I feel the same way. I like love y-"

I gasped, I could feel myself beginning to get nauseous again. Loud thunder clapped from outside and shook me. I spun myself away from Nicky, reaching for the trash bin at the foot of the couch. I picked it up, lowering myself over it in the same second I began throwing up once again.

A similar sequence of events continued for the next several hours. As the storm blew through the city, I vomited up an entire day's worth of food and alcohol. Nicky was always there, supporting me, holding me, cleaning me up when I needed it. I was so grateful for him. More than I could ever express with words.

It was nearing three a.m. by the time the majority of the sickness subsided. Both Nicky and I were exhausted, taking turns laying on each other as the other napped. We were both always startled awake by a vomiting spell, but, as time went on, they became fewer and the tiredness of us both became more pronounced.

I finally worked up the courage to set down the trash bin around three thirty, feeling confident I wouldn't throw up for at least a good while. Nicky smiled sleepily at me when he noticed this, offering me the most space on the couch so I could drape my legs across his. I felt too unsteady to move to the bed just yet, so I did as he asked, balancing my head back against the stiff arm of the couch.

"You feeling better?" he wondered, rubbing my legs from knees to ankles.

I yawned. "I think I am. I can think straighter at least. I hope I didn't say anything weird earlier."

"Well, you did tell me you loved me."

I snorted through my nose, pressing my fists onto my eyelids. "Oh, lord! I'm so sorry. I didn't mean to make you uncomfortable. I wasn't thinking. I just care about you and wish I could make all the hurt go away. I feel like I owe you so much. Sympathizing, and badly at that, does nothing to make up for it."

"Kasi, don't do that. You don't owe me anything. All I want is for you to be healthy. Take care of yourself and you'll help me, alright?"

"As long as you promise to do the same. From now on, okay?"

"Agreed. Starting with your running nose." he teased me, bending over to hand me a fresh tissue.

I grabbed it, wiping my nose gently, then tossing it aside in the direction of the trash bin. Nicky stayed still, leaning over me, examining my face with an apprehensive curiosity. I smiled at him, examining him back, searching his eyes for things he did not wish to say. What I saw in them, though, was more than the pain I expected. It shocked me, thoroughly, but I saw clear longing in them. Desperate desire, even.

I blinked slowly, trying to collect my thoughts. I could smell him so close to me, his strong, husky scent that I'd come to associate with safety and comfort over time. Just the smell of him put a coating on the inside of my skin, protecting me like a suit of armor. I let myself imagine for just a moment that the smell of me did the same for him. But, then I realized that I probably smelled like alcohol and vomit most of the time I was around him. That was no comfort to anyone.

I stared back into his face, searching it for an answer to my unspoken question. I could feel his chest expanding and retracting against my thighs as he hovered over me. I noticed that he'd begun to lean even farther in, one of his arms sliding across the back of the couch closer to me. My breath caught in my lungs, my heart fluttering.

Was he communicating to me now what I'd been selfishly wanting for so long? Was it wrong for me to let him this close?

I didn't know what to do.

"Nicky?"

"Yeah?" His breath was so hot on my skin.

"Is it wrong for me to ask you to kiss me?

His eyes welled with tears.

I was about to flee. I thought I'd made a mistake. I thought I'd interpreted wrong. I thought my conscience had worked its magic out into the universe, preventing this abnormal, selfish longing from being fulfilled.

But, then he did kiss me.

He took my face in one of his hands and gently pressed his lips into mine. He kissed me so deeply I forgot where I was. I could only feel traces of reality as his fingers moved to the nape of my neck, holding me steady while he continued to deliver me the greatest gift. To fulfill a great act of selflessness for my benefit.

Once the initial shock wore off, I managed to kiss him back. I worked my lips against his soft mouth, feeling the taste of him on my tongue. I felt my hands move on their own, reaching up to take hold of his shirt, clutching him closer to me still. His body weight fell heavier and heavier into me, nearly crushing me with his embrace, but I didn't mind. The feel of him close to me was overwhelming. I didn't want it to end.

He pulled away first, wiping away tears from his cheeks as he did. He then bowed his head and kissed the tears off of mine. We stayed resting cheek to cheek for a moment, soaking up each other as much as we could. I ran my good hand through his hair, holding onto his neck to keep him from leaving for a minute longer.

"Kasi?"

"Yeah?"

"Do you know how long I've wanted to do that?"

"You wanted to?"

He sat up, anger twisting onto his face.

"Yes? I wouldn't have if I didn't."

"I just thought-"

"Just thought you were the only one?"

"I guess."

"Well, you're wrong. I've wanted to do that from the moment I laid eyes on you. In a different world, I probably would've asked you for your number after I bought those stupid cigarettes."

"I wish it could've been simple like that."

"Nothing's ever simple."

"No, it's not."

We looked at each other for another long moment, then Nicky sat up the rest of the way. He rubbed his eyes, standing up and walking towards the bed. He collapsed onto it, sprawling out like a starfish.

"You should probably take a shower, Kasi. It might make you feel better." he mumbled through the blankets.

"Good idea." I sighed, swinging my legs around and heading for the bathroom.

Before I shut the door behind me, however, I saw him get up and go to the balcony of our room, widening the curtains and stepping out into the rainy night. He had a lit cigarette in his hand and bent forward over the railing, blowing smoke out into the empty air. The way his shoulders pressed together as he loosened his body made him seem so ruggedly tough, and yet, the way his head lolled downwards reminded me that he was just as fragile as I was and just as in need of love.

Chapter 12

I stripped down to my bare ass on the mat in front of the shower, then slowly and methodically pulled back the curtain to get inside. The water burned my skin as I stepped into it, but I didn't have the energy to turn around and adjust the temperature. I simply stood there and let it pound into my back, grinding deeper and deeper into my flesh until I just felt nothing at all. Leaning my head back into the steam, I wet my hair, closing my eyes as the water rushed over my face. The partly smeared and partly dried blood still on my upper lip ran down my chest and pooled below me in a dark, red mess.

There were no conscious thoughts in my head as I felt the weight of my feet sink into the porcelain. I could only feel physically and barely at that. A slow smile grew as I remembered Nicky kissing me. The thought of him against my body made me tense with a chill, my heart finding peace despite the disaster that my life was. I was so lucky to have him. Even if my feelings felt selfish, I couldn't deny it was a miracle anybody would ever care about me. My whole life I had just wished that for once someone would love me as much as I loved them because I couldn't keep myself from fucking falling in love. Not to say what we felt for each other was love, but it was pretty close.

My thoughts centered around Nicky made me realize something as I stood there disappearing from the world. Something insane about myself and about him. If I could care about Nicky, if I could want the world for him and want to protect him and make his life better, then I could do the same for myself. I could love myself. I could take care of my mind and my body. He deserved that. I deserved that. He shouldn't have to take care of me. He was right. The best way to take care of him was to take care of myself.

And, it was at that moment that I decided something. Truly, like a miracle, it entered my very skin, seeping through me like some contagious disease, willing hopes and desires in me that I'd never entertained before. This wretched night contributed to the decision, but ultimately Nicky had inspired me. I knew it would be hell. I knew it might even kill me. But, I had to try. I had never felt stronger about anything in my life before. I had never wanted it more. I had never wanted it, period. Until now.

I wanted to try to get sober. For Nicky. And for me.

After a while, my eyes unglossed themselves as I began to feel a whole body quiver of nausea. To a degree, it felt like the beginnings of a usual hangover, but the way it shook and dizzied me was unsettling. The shower started spinning around me, the water becoming heavier and denser against my back. The room suddenly seemed to be shrinking, growing smaller and smaller until I drowned.

In the midst of the hallucination, I doubled over and vomited onto the floor. The mucus and acid and now blood trickled through my toes as it fell towards the drain. A tingling sensation rose in my throat, causing me to cough loudly and violently. I gasped for air, but all of it in the bathroom seemed to have been sucked out like a vacuum.

Scrambling with unexpected fear, I wrenched open the shower curtain and tripped out over the tub ledge, not bothering to turn the water off. I launched myself to the toilet and sat myself down, hugging my knees desperately gasping still. An uneasy panic started to set in as my stomach began to twist itself into a ghastly, uncomfortable knot, which sent moans out through my clenched teeth.

As the pain worsened, the nausea returned, the air slipped away, and my logical mind disappeared. I became so overcome that I passed onto the floor. I only remembered falling to my knees, then waking up a second later to a banging sound at the door. Nicky was pounding his way in, shouting words I couldn't understand, shaking the doorknob with immeasurable force. In a matter of seconds, he broke the lock, stormed in, and squatted down next to me.

I saw his face shrivel with...well I don't know what it was as his eyes moved from my helpless face to the floor below me. Tears rolled down my cheeks as I looked down too and saw a pool of blood between my legs.

It all made sense. The nausea, the pain, the anxiety, the hallucinating. My period mixed with the copious amounts of alcohol I'd consumed plus a severely injured hand really fucked with my body. I hadn't had one in so long, I wasn't sure why it was happening now.

"Shit." I whispered as I watched huge clots of my uterine lining flow into the sopping mess that now stained the floor.

The blood soaked into the grout and flowed along the lines, reaching a wider and wider area as I dripped water into it, making a lovely vile soup. The clots were large and thick, and I knew it was because, for years, the increased amount of toxins in my system had been fucking with my estrogen and making me skip periods. The build up of my uterine wall was due to burst soon and now here it was, soaking Nicky's socks.

"C'mere." he reached out and grabbed both my arms, lifting me slowly off the ground.

I began to cry heavily as he scooped my legs out from under me and carried me out of the bathroom, laying me gently on the cool sheets of the bed. I heard him go behind me and shut the shower water off, then he returned only a second later, placing a towel behind my head to keep my now freezing hair off my neck. Through slivers, I watched him walk around the other side of the bed and climb in next to me, drawing the blankets up over both of us.

Scooting over closer and closer, he drew one of my legs over his, sliding his hand behind my back, so he could press me into his chest. I could feel myself bleeding into his leg that was tucked between my thighs, but I had a feeling he didn't care.

"Close your eyes." Nicky purred, pressing my face into his shoulder.

The sweatshirt he wore smelled of him so intensely and his temperature was so different to the iciness I felt within myself. I wanted him to consume me in every way possible. My heart rate had already started to decrease and the deep sinking pain was only a distant memory. In his arms, I felt so utterly safe that I could simply pass away and not be scared at all. I'd never thought it possible for someone to care for me this much. I never thought I could care for someone this much.

If this is what it means to love someone, I don't think I've ever loved anyone before. But, I really think I do now.

When I woke the next morning, Nicky was still beside me, sleeping on his back, his chest rising and falling with his shallow breaths. I'd been wrapped up in his sweatshirt that had blood and what I assumed were vomit stains on the sleeves. Instinctively, I reached my hand down in between my legs and felt a towel spread there. It was soaked with my warm blood, but it was not so soaked to make me cold.

I rolled over towards the bathroom door and saw the mess on the floor had been cleaned too, and there was not a single hint of smell anywhere in the room. He'd taken such good care of me all night when I genuinely hadn't deserved it.

Suddenly, an arm draped over mine, squeezing me gently.

"Hey." I whispered.

Nicky murmured something back to me, tiredly, pressing his lips against my neck. My breath caught and goose bumps trickled down my spine.

"You alright?" he asked, mouthing the tiny gap behind my ear.

"Yeah."

Nicky's arm that gripped me, hugged tighter, his legs curling up behind me to spoon. I could feel *all* of him pressed against me and my heart stopped. He wasn't excited in that sense, but the way his body felt formed around mine sent butterflies in between my thighs. I knew Nicky couldn't have known he made me feel this way, and I wasn't entirely sure if I wanted to feel this way. I didn't want our connection to be born of trauma. I didn't want him to do this for me just to make me feel better. Apart from the fact that it definitely did, I didn't want him to sacrifice his own feelings just to ease mine. I couldn't do that to him.

And, I couldn't let him become yet another addiction to me. I wasn't sure how to keep myself from letting it morph into that. What was he to me if not the beginnings of another dependent lifeforce?

"Nicky?"

"Mmm?" he mumbled into my neck.

His breath was hot against me, searing my skin. Subconsciously, I grabbed his hand that was gently laid over my stomach, holding it in mine.

"Do you...I don't know how to ask this? We're *friends*, right?"

He chuckled. "Of course."

"But-"

"But, what?"

I turned around to face him, locking my gaze in his gorgeous eyes. I stared at him for a long moment, then reached up, kissing him tenderly. He didn't react at first, only allowing me to kiss him without any efforts of his own.

"What does that mean to you?" I asked, breaking away.

"What do you want that to mean?"

"It doesn't matter what I want. It's you I'm worried about. I want to know what you feel."

He smirked at me, releasing my hand that was still clasped in his and sliding it up my bare chest over the covers. As he reached the base of my breast, I gasped aloud, feeling my shoulders tense.

"What it means to me," he whispered. "Is beyond anything you could ever imagine. You have no idea. I told you last night when, respectfully, you were at your absolute worst. I still felt the same way then that I feel now. That I've felt for a while. I care about you in lots of different ways. In many more ways than are just friendly."

My lips spread into a slow smile, my heart convulsing in my chest. I rolled back over, afraid I would start to cry. Nicky's hand didn't move even though I did, and our bodies seemed to move as one as I tried to shy away. Nicky's mouth followed suit, finding a sensitive spot behind my ear, brushing it with his tongue. I giggled a bit at the feeling, beginning to realize just how much I wanted him. My mind clear and my heart full.

With a burst of courage, I took his hand on my chest once again, grasping the back of it. He stopped playing with my ear, shocked a little at the movement, waiting for me to make a move. Steadily, I began drawing it higher and higher, until both our hands rested gently on top of one of my breasts.

"Is this alright?" I asked him, unsure if I was being too bold.

His hand began to clamp down in a squeeze as his mouth met my head. "Absolutely perfect."

His tender lips moved across my hairline, stopping at the base of my ear, his teeth nibbling on the lobe. I guided the movement of his hand, massaging my tit with sluggish motions, my heart beating faster and faster.

Without entirely knowing what I was doing, I turned quickly, taking his face in my hands, reaching my own forwards. I caught his bottom lip as he went to back away, biting onto it. I pushed him upwards, then back down onto his back, leaning my body against his chest. He grabbed one of my thighs, pulling me up on top of him, shoving his tongue in my mouth. Before I caught myself, I moaned into him, feeling him take both my hips in his hands, grinding me against his own.

"Have I ever told you how beautiful you are?" he breathed, sitting up and wrapping his arms around my back, arching me into his chest.

"Have I ever told you how beautiful you are?"

"Oh, Kas." he laughed, reaching down to kiss my neck.

"Do you wanna go further?" I whispered, leaning away to look straight into his eyes.

"Are you sure?"

"Yes."

"You're not feeling too sick? We don't have to do this now, we can wai-"

"No," I kissed him hard, cutting him off. "I want this."

He gave me a crooked smile, then flipped me around, tackling me onto my back. He took my good wrist, holding it above my head with one hand, groping my chest with the other. With his sweet lips, he bent low and sucked the other tit, keeping my legs from squirming with his own.

"Kasi, you deserve this." he gasped, gliding back up to meet my mouth.

"So do you." I groaned, my breath raspy.

The hand he'd been using to hold my wrist released me suddenly, and he let his fingers drape across my face as he worked them down my body. Our eyes locked and I stared directly into him, watching his grinning, cautious face as his light fingers traced the outer lining of my side. He lowered them farther and farther until he reached the edge of my hip.

I moaned again, squinting my eyes, but keeping them focused on him.

"Are you sure?"

"Yes." I breathed, my eyes welling up with happy tears. "Please."

His lip turned up on one side, then his fingers dropped low and slid inside me, his thumb pressing firmly into my clit. I inhaled sharply, unable to stop myself from watching the pleasure in Nicky's eyes. Any momentary insecurity I might've had about being on my period was lost in that second, seeing the way he rallied at being able to make me feel something I'd never been able to make myself feel.

His movements started steady at first, but then increased. Both his hands were working tirelessly, one still on my breast. I reached up to kiss him, taking his lips for only a moment before the moans rising from deep in my throat made it hard to breathe. Nicky didn't let me escape, though, grabbing my lip in his teeth.

"Nicky, oh lord." I shouted, feeling my back arch towards him.

The sensation was wild. I felt so tensely rigid with desire and yet I felt totally relaxed. I could feel my muscles begin to loosen, my legs and arms becoming limper and airier as if they were beginning to float. Then, as I felt myself getting closer to feeling that had been building in between my legs, Nicky suddenly stopped. He removed his fingers and released my tit, sitting right up in front of me. I watched in fearful awe, sad that he'd stopped so soon and worried I'd been too much.

My confused expression only received a full hearty laugh as Nicky took his shirt in both hands, raising it above his head. He wiped his fingers in it, then threw it across the room, his chest gleaming with sweat, the gold chain he wore around his neck reflecting the moisture over his tattoos.

In an instant, he was back on top of me, kissing me fiercely. I seized handfuls of his hair with my good hand, gripping his locks tightly, wanting every bit of him. I could feel a hard bulge in his pants now as he grinded into me harder and faster. The feel of him brought back the rage in my vagina and I could feel my clit hardening once more, the mere taste of him overwhelming me to my core. My hands slid down his back, grabbing him, pulling him, trying whatever I could to bring him closer.

He jumped away abruptly, leaning himself over the side of the bed.

"What's wrong?" I asked him, sitting up.

He laughed, fumbling with something he'd plucked from the floor. "Condom."

I watched him pull the packet from his wallet, then open it along the seam. I turned away, not wanting to make him uncomfortable, but I heard his pants unzip, a bit of struggle, then I felt his hand on my shoulder.

He pressed his lips into the side of my shoulder from behind me, taking my neck in his hand. With his other hand, he reached around my stomach, holding me gently while he sucked on my skin. I whined softly in my throat, leaning my head into him, enjoying the ease of the moment.

Subtly, he began to move around me, crossing his leg over me, so he was on top of me completely. I could feel his dick, draped across my inner thigh. It was throbbing, beating just about as hard as his heart in his chest. I found his lips, kissing him thoroughly.

Throughout my life, I'd only ever experienced and associated sex with fast-paced dramatic urgency, but Nicky was different. Every movement he made was slow and methodical. I wasn't scared of him. I didn't brace for pain. He prepared me for him, he made me feel real pleasure. The very principle of the way he treated me turned me on with insanity.

I breathed into his open mouth as he placed his thumb in the crook of my pelvis, balancing himself and then shoving himself into me with careful gentility.

I felt a strong sound rise from the base of my chest as his dick thrust deeper inside me. He laughed, moving away from my face to watch me as my face contorted with the thrill.

From there, he continued working his body into me, starting steadily, then beginning a quick, strong, heavy motion, bending over and breathing raucously into my face for a minute or two. Then he chuckled suddenly, rocking back onto his knees. He drew me up towards him, then wrapped my legs around his back. I grabbed onto his head, holding onto his hair as he took my hips in his hands.

"Is this okay?" he asked, his sweaty palms clinging to my ass.

"Yes." I breathed, mouthing his neck just below the jawline.

He whimpered as I touched him, laying me back down again, dropping his hips farther down onto me. He placed one of his hands across my lower stomach, pressing his palm into my abdomen. I practically screamed, feeling a pleasure so unreal and so seemingly unachievable. He seemed to enjoy the way I reacted, falling against me heavily. Nearly his whole body weight was on me then, reminding me of that special moment we'd shared last night. It made it almost hard to breathe except for the constant release of moans and grunts, but I loved it.

"Does this feel good?" he asked, gasping into my neck, thrusting one of his hands into the pillow behind me to support himself.

"Yes." I cried out, feeling more tears begin to fall down my cheeks.

"Good. You deserve every second of this."

His pace was slowing, his voice exhausted. He pulled out unexpectedly, struggling to catch his breath. I wasn't sure if he had finished, but it was obvious he had little strength to continue. I couldn't blame him.

"Do you want to stop?" I wondered, massaging the back of his head.

His dick was still pulsating between my thighs, just as hard as it had been when we started.

"No, I'm sorry. Just give me a minute." he panted, laying his head into my shoulder.

"Hold on. Sit up." I plead, pushing myself forward.

I watched him wearily lift himself backwards onto his butt, sitting there with his legs out. He gawked at me as I shifted onto my knees and started crawling towards him, sweat pouring from my forehead. He smiled, lowering himself back onto his hands. I positioned myself on top of him, crossing my arms behind his head and pressing my tits against his face. His tongue reached out, circling one of my nipples, shallow breaths flowing out into my chest.

Starting very slowly, I began grinding against him, raising and lowering my hips, gliding my wetness against him. With my entire tit in his mouth, he groaned out, reaching his arms around me, enveloping my whole body. Being gentle to the extent of nearly teasing, I took one of my hands, tracing it down his chest. I went farther and farther down until I reached the base of his dick, taking it firmly with my fingers.

"Kasi!" he shouted, his eyes rolling back into his head.

"Does it feel good? Do you want me to stop?"

"Yes, fuck, you're incredible! Please, don't stop!"

I slipped it inside me, taking Nicky's hair in my free hand, pulling it backwards away from me. His body followed my motion, and he fell straight onto his back, his hands clutched against my hips and ass for support. I dropped my own low onto his chest and began rocking myself back and forth against him. He guided the pace with his hands, pushing and pulling me as I drove myself into him harder and faster.

The intensity and sexual pleasure of the moment was no match for the immense emotional gratification that encompassed me. I'd never felt a better feeling than being completely and utterly vulnerable in this bed. I was disgustingly myself. And I was adored. I didn't feel like I deserved it at all.

I could tell we were both getting close.

I'd admit it any day, I was a selfish person. I only ever really did things for myself, but watching how much pleasure I gave Nicky, totally railed me. Just the look on his face was enough to kill me, strip me down to my bear bones and crumble onto the floor in a heap. I could've finished right then just watching him, grinning and groaning, tensing from the pleasure. He was perfection before my eyes. The odd thing was though, I almost knew he felt the exact same way about me. By now I had to believe it. All he'd ever done since the moment I'd met him in that god forsaken Shell was take care of me. In every way. And now, I had an opportunity to do the very same for him. I wanted to take care of him. I wanted to love him.

Suddenly, Nicky sat up, taking me in his arms again. He started smiling and laughing so brightly and passionately, more tears began to fall down my face. His soft fingers maneuvered their way up my back, sending tingles down my spine. As they reached my neck, they grabbed on gently, holding me still.

"You're so beautiful." he said.

And it was then that I truly felt it.

Chapter 13

"Oh, fuck, Nicky." I sighed, leaning back down onto my back. He followed me, laying his head against my stomach, breathing loudly into my skin. I grabbed onto his hair measuredly petting him. He hugged my middle, drawing his hands up and around me. I felt so safe in his arms like I never had before. It was a kind of beautiful, vulnerable safety. It took my breath away, honestly, melting my insides like molten glass. It felt as if Nicky had reached inside my body and cradled my heart in his hands, protecting it, healing it, sealing it of its many fissures and ruptures.

It wasn't just because of the sex. It wasn't just because he'd made me feel things no guy has ever made me feel before. The way he treated me, treated my body, treated my soul was unlike anything I'd ever experienced. It wasn't the kind of care that my parents showed me, which felt to me almost like obligation and exhaustion. It was the kind of deep affection of wanting someone and wanting them to be well so badly that it literally feels like you're going to fall forever if they're not. It wasn't that he needed me. Or that I needed him. It was a mutual want of the other, knowing both of our lives were only better with the other in it.

I grasped Nicky's shoulders and brought him up closer to my chest. He snuggled himself into my neck, kissing me down my jaw. I tucked one of my legs between his, curling myself up so I could wrap my other arm around him. He met my mouth as I turned, reaching my back with his hand and drawing me closer to him.

We kissed for a while, nothing intense, just kissing each other in different places, simply enjoying the presence of the other. I wanted to feel every inch of him. I wanted to allow my feelings for him to flow through my lips as I kissed his chest, his neck, his nose, his eyes, his hands, his fingers, his stomach, his hips as he did the same to mine. Although, his kiss felt more like a butterfly's to me. So soft and with so much intention. It was strange to feel so enamored. It was strange to watch him on top of me, kissing me from my belly button to my neck, telling me how amazing and beautiful I was. I don't think anyone had ever felt that way about me before. I don't think I'd ever felt that way about someone.

I wanted him so much. More than just physically. I knew, though, it wouldn't be easy to keep it from becoming yet another chemically-induced trap. I knew what I wanted to be for him. I knew what he deserved. I knew I could be what he deserved. But, I'd have to make a choice. A hard choice. After this morning, though, I knew I was ready to make it.

"Nicky?"

"Yeah?" he brushed my arm from my elbow to my shoulder, gliding his fingers up and down my skin.

"I want to get sober."

He sat up to look me in the eyes, his whole face lightened. "Really?"

"Yes, but I want to tell you why first."

"Yeah, okay."

"It's because of you, mainly. You made me realize how worthy I am. For such a long time, I didn't think I deserved to be taken care of. I didn't even want anyone else to take care of me. I couldn't let even myself take care of me. That's kind of where the self-destructive behavior came from. I didn't care if I lived or died. It just never mattered to me,

"And, I owe most of that to someone who hurt me a long time ago. I was a freshman in highschool when I met him. He was older, popular, everything I thought I wanted in a guy. He was one of the first people to ever show me attention. I loved it. I felt special. But, he didn't care how I felt. He knew he could break me. He found it fun. He manipulated me into trusting him and wanting him, then he raped me on a dare his friends made him. I remember him taking me out on a drive. I thought we were just going to get ice cream, but he stopped on the side of the road about halfway there. He drove down into a ditch beside the road, parked the car, then looked me straight in the eyes and said 'I wanna fuck you.'

"I told him I wasn't sure if I was ready for that. Then, he said I was being hypocritical because of all the times I'd made sex-related jokes or we'd phone-fucked. He said I'd led him on and that if I didn't intend to give it to him, I shouldn't have ever agreed to go out with him. I felt so awful in that moment. So, I agreed. We climbed in the backseat and immediately he began ripping my clothes off. I wasn't prepared for how aggressive he was, but he just kept repeating 'Fuck, I'm so horny'. I remember he grabbed one of my tits so hard it hurt, and I shouted out that I wanted to stop,

"He wasn't going to take no for an answer, though. He let go of my chest and used both hands to choke me. He pinned me down to the seat of the truck, hitting my head hard against the door. I think I must've blacked out when he slammed me into the handle because the next thing I remember is him absolutely pummeling me with the roughest, most painful penetration ever. I tried to scream, but he still had one hand around my neck, so it was hard enough for me to breathe let alone yell. He came inside me, never bothering to put on a condom. He drove me home after, then we never spoke again. His friends later told me that it had been them that had made him do it. They laughed about it, reminiscing about it in front of me like it was the funniest thing to them,

"The worst part of everything was he knew exactly what he was doing. Dare or no dare. If he really wanted me as bad as he said he did, he would've asked. He wouldn't have driven me into a ditch, turning the car lights off so no one would see us, then not take no for an answer. He had planned on hurting me. And, it amounted to nothing. I was too ashamed to report it and his friends certainly didn't. He graduated the next year, so I never saw him again. That was that."

Nicky didn't say a word, just stared at me with wide eyes.

"I blamed myself. I thought it was my fault. His friends, at least, made it seem like it was. Rape was common enough. I mean it's 2002. Most of my friends had been in one way or another. I wasn't the first one and I certainly won't be the last. I thought the way it made me feel afterwards was abnormal. So, I internalized. I wanted to hide that part of myself from everyone, including me. I truly believed after that that I was worthless. Until today, I never knew that sex could be slow and sweet and feel good. I always associated it with pain. I haven't had sex since I was raped. You were the first person I ever truly wanted to be with like that,"

"But, I didn't know you back then. I didn't know I could be worth something. So, that's when the drinking started. Even back in highschool, I'd take liquor from my dad's stash and drink and drink until I got sick. It almost made me feel better to know I was destroying myself. I never really drank for the high or the happiness. I drank because I thought that was all I deserved. Then, my parents got divorced and my childhood got messy. I was constantly switching between houses. There was no consistency in my life. Except for alcohol. I was miserable all the time. I hated everything."

I grinned at Nicky. "You showed me, though. You taught me what it felt like to be happy. Even in this miserable, fucking nightmare, I think I'm the happiest I've ever been in my entire life. It has been hell, but I don't regret a single moment that I've spent with you. Selfishly, I don't want that to end. I want to sober up and I want to live. For you. And for me."

Nicky took one of his hands, tracing different features of my face with his fingertips. He then reached down and kissed me, softly. When he moved away from me again, he placed a hand over my heart, pressing down against me.

"I love you. Is that crazy?" he whispered.

"No. I think I love you, too."

"Think?" he chuckled.

"No," I shook my head. "I do love you. I love you so much."

~~~~~~

"I need a shower." Nicky murmured in my ear half an hour later.

We'd been cuddling for a while, drifting in and out of sleep, but I agreed. A shower was necessary. For both of us truthfully.

"Could I join you?" I asked, shy despite the position I was in.

He laughed into my hair. "Of course, darling."

He rolled over, standing up and stretching away from me. I followed, crawling out of the bed and onto my feet. It was cold outside the cover of the blankets, but the promise of Nicky's warm skin just minutes away made it bearable. I could hear him turn the shower on in the bathroom, but I wasn't quite ready to meet him. Instead, I picked up the towel that had been between my legs last night, drying myself off with it. I'd been free-bleeding for hours. I was a sticky, stinky mess.

"Kasi? You ready?" Nicky called for me.

"Yeah, I'm just cleaning up a little."

"What? That's what the shower's for."

"I just don't want you to think I'm gross."

The bathroom door was open slightly, Nicky having moved it to get to the shower, but as the words left my mouth, it jolted open. Nicky stood there, naked except for socks, spots of my blood on his own thighs, scars on his chest from the fight in the Shell and maybe even from the bar yesterday, frowning at me. I realized how stupid I sounded. At least, how stupid I must've sounded to Nicky.

"Kas, you're the farthest thing from gross. Any embarrassment you might have in your head right now, I just want you to know that I love it. I want it. It makes me so hot for you."

"But-"

"No "buts". I've felt so gross for so long, too. I haven't showered nearly as often as I should've. I haven't been able to do my hair or brush my teeth or put on a nice smelling cologne. I was so afraid to tell you how I felt because I really thought you were disgusted by me. I'm just a big smelly guy, who knows he's not as sexy as most other men out there. But, I don't think you think that. At least, I hope you don't."

"No, I don't, that's not true, you're not-"

"See my point? We've been with each other and seen each other during the most raw, unshielded events of our lives. And neither of us have run away. That means something, doesn't it?"

"You're right. I guess I just am still struggling with the idea of you genuinely caring about me. I don't feel like I deserve it."

Nicky took a few steps over to me, taking the towel from my hands and throwing it behind me onto the bed. He then took my arms, wrapping them around his middle so he could hug me.

"Kasi, you do deserve it. You deserve it more than anyone else in the world. I will do my best to prove that to you every day we have left together."

"And, I hope to do the same for you. You deserve so much, Nicky. You're such an extraordinary person. I hope to be worthy of someone you deserve."

"You already are. I'm so lucky that a wonderful girl like you thinks I'm even half the man I am."

"I don't agree, but I don't think I can argue with you."

"Nope."

I sighed heavily, then let myself be led into the bathroom. Nicky threw his socks off and climbed into the shower first, helping me up after him. I was still a bit weak, my hand aching, my stomach growling. But once the warm water hit my back, my tensed muscles relaxed, the steam cleansing my lungs.

Nicky's hands immediately went to my hair, wetting it, but keeping the water out of my eyes. I expected him to finish with that, but, a second later, he was pouring shampoo onto my head, massaging it into my scalp. I hadn't imagined this being what "showering" with him was, but I couldn't complain. His love language was very obviously acts of service, and I very intentionally remembered that. I was prepared to devote myself to doing whatever it took to make our dynamic mutual. I hadn't always been the best at it. Selfishly, I'd enjoyed the feeling of someone taking care of me for the first time in my life. But, Nicky deserved that as well.

Once the shampoo had been washed clean from my hair, I turned myself around to grab the bottle from Nicky, pouring some out into my hand.

"What are you doing?" he chuckled.

"I'm trying to help you, now bend down, I can't reach."

He stooped low for me, leaning his head towards my chest. Clumsily, I spread the shampoo through his hair, trying to copy what he did, moving my fingers methodically against him. The feeling his tender touch gave me had healing powers, and I wanted to replicate that for him. I wanted him to feel the physical aspect of my promise of being worthy of him.

As I reached the back of his neck, a soft groan sounded in his throat. It was very noticeably a sound of pleasure, and I took that as a good sign. That I was doing this right. His hands very sneakily moved to my hips, drawing me into him. His head bent even lower, his sudsy hair brushing against my neck. Then, I felt his lips on one of my nipples.

I didn't stop massaging him as he began mouthing me, allowing him to hold me to him. I couldn't help moaning a little against the back of my own lips as he sucked, the warm steam and water rushing against my back, heating up the room.

"Nicky?" I finally said.

"Mmm?" he mumbled into my skin.

"Let's rinse your hair."

"Ugh, fine!" he growled, straightening himself and switching positions with me so he was facing the water.

I hugged him from behind as he washed the shampoo out, pressing my lips to his bare back. Once all the soap had washed away, I turned him back around, kissing him underneath his chin. My tongue subconsciously reached out beyond me, licking the water off his neck, advancing down his chest, running up, down, and across it. When I returned to his neck, he grabbed my face with both his hands, planting a mouthy kiss on my lips. I felt his own tongue thrust its way into my mouth, water and saliva mixing.

I slid my good hand up his sopping chest, wrapping my arm around the back of his head. His own hands moved down my body, one resting on the small of my back, the other squeezing one of my ass cheeks as he moaned into my mouth.

"Is this okay?" he breathed against my lips.

"Mhm."

"Kasi, you sure?"

I opened my eyes and saw him staring at me. "Yeah, it feels good." I smiled at him.

He laughed back at me, diving back in to kiss me again. In only a moment, though, he pulled away. "Hey, I want to tell you something."

I nodded to him, drawing one of his arms up in my direction, holding his hand in mine and kissing its knuckles.

"Look at me real quick."

I found his eyes.

"I promise you...I promise you with my whole damn soul that I will *never* treat you like that guy did in highschool. I will *never* let you be treated like that by anyone else either. I'd rather die than let that happen. It wasn't your fault and I'm so fucking sorry."

"Thank you." I mumbled, my eyes burning from incoming tears. No one had ever said anything like that to me before. I'd never been made a promise so sweet and genuine and that I honestly believed. The words were few but they meant everything to me.

"Hey, hey, it's okay," Nicky cooed, noticing the growing redness of my eyes. He took his thumbs and wiped the tears, holding my cheeks like they were made of glass. "We should condition your hair. All that dye is going to dry it out."

I giggled under my breath, fighting sobs. "Okay, professional. How do you even know all of this?"

"I have a little sister, remember?"

"And she taught you this?"

"We learned it together. My mom's psychotic. She never would've taught her."

"I'm sorry."

"Thank you. But, turn around, let me put this on."

Nicky conditioned my hair, then I argued with him until he let me do his too. My favorite part, though, was when we both got to scrub ourselves with the body soap, washing away days and days of grime. I still had blood under my fingernails from my hand, crusted there having seeped deep into my pores. When we were clean, it was like taking a breath of fresh air. Almost like being reborn. We were discovering new, untarnished versions of ourselves by washing away all that still tied us to the past.

I stepped out of the shower feeling like a different person. My heart was full, my body clean, and my life more uncertain than ever. For the time being, though, I had one constant. Nicky. And he had me.

An hour later, we decided it was time for us to go. Nicky packed our clothes and gathered our extra things while I stripped the bed of the bloody sheets and attempted to wash them in the tub. I felt embarrassed by my mess, afraid for even Nicky to see it, but again he didn't mind. He even asked me if I needed things for my period. I told him I'd manage with stuffing tissues into my underwear until we could get to the store, but the fact that he even asked at all was surprising to me. It was such a good feeling. There was nothing I had to hide from him. He now knew me better than anyone else on the whole planet. I liked that.

We left about midday, taking to the streets once more. Our first mission was to get me some period products, so we stopped at a small convenience store just down the road from the hotel. I grabbed a box of pads and Nicky bought some snacks for us to have. We were desperately running out of money. I'd used the last of my cash bulk on the hotel and us having restaurant meals was really draining our resources.

We only had one option. We'd have to stop at an atm.

The problem was that it was very likely our credit and debit cards were being tracked. Anywhere we made a purchase or used an atm would alert the card companies of our whereabouts. As soon as we used them, we wouldn't have a lot of time to ditch before the police came searching for us. It would have to be quick.

Our plan was to find another bus station, hoping they had an atm inside. It wasn't safe for us to go back to anywhere we'd been before, so we just had to keep moving forward. We asked a few strangers on our way if there was another bus station and they directed us without thinking. I had been anxious to approach anyone, but, for the most part, people didn't seem to care very much. It wasn't like every person had their eyes out for us and was ready to report us at any given moment. I was grateful for that.

I thought back to the woman at the last bus station in Charleston. She was so sweet and innocent, and yet, I'd lied to her. I'd blatantly lied to her. It wasn't right. None of what had happened lately was right. Even though we were still running, I hadn't given up hope that I'd find an opportunity to turn myself in. I wanted to do it to protect Nicky so badly. But, I also didn't know if I could afford to lose him.

"Look, 'atm inside' sign." Nicky said, crossing us to the other side of the street towards the bus station.

I saw it too, hanging in one of the windows, glowing a bit from the lights behind it. There were quite a few more people inside this bus station than the last we'd been at, but I knew I could only duck my head, hide my hand, and keep walking.

There was a line to the atm, so we waited off to the side a little, pretending to shuffle through our bags.

"How's your hand?" Nicky asked me, rubbing his palm against my shoulder.

I shrugged. "It aches, I guess."

"The bleeding still fine?"

"Well, I did probably fuck up the bandage when I showered with it, so it is a little loose. I can feel it bleeding from time to time, but not much."

"I hope I didn't...hurt it earlier."

I smiled at him, nudging his side with my arm. "I would've told you."

"You better. And, in the future, always tell me if I make you uncomfortable or hurt you, okay?"

"I will. But, you never have. I promise."

He reached the rest of the way around my back to hug me, pressing me in close to his side. His expected warmth surrounded me with its protection, sending good goosebumps down my arms. I held a lot less guilt now allowing myself to let him love me this way. Nothing had changed. I hadn't fixed anything. But, we'd both shared a burden with each other and both provided something to whatever this connection was between us. It wasn't just one-sided anymore. I thought, at least, I was finally helping him, too. Trying to, at least.

"Are you in line?" an elderly gentleman asked us, stooped over a bit with age.

"Yes, but you can go ahead of us." I told him, throwing my hood back a small amount to show him a grin.

"No, no. I insist. I have time."

I looked to Nicky for guidance. His eyes agreed with my thoughts. We couldn't refuse this man. We thanked him, then moved our way up to the atm. I pulled out my debit card, turning it over in my hands a few times.

"Nicky," I whispered, suddenly thinking of something. "What if it doesn't let us get anything out? What if it locks the card, sharing the location anyway? It might alert the people here or something."

He stared, reflectively, for a moment, chewing on his bottom lip. "We don't know unless we try. We don't have many other options."

He was right. We didn't have any other options. We were virtually out of money, and we needed to get out of Kennewick.

I inhaled a deep breath, plunging my card into the slot. The screen was frozen for a second, then my account information came up. I entered the security code, then punched the button until $200 worth of cash started spilling out of the machine. I almost cheered aloud at the fact that sirens weren't blaring all around us, but I couldn't react. To anyone watching, this had to be a normal interaction. We couldn't seem suspicious.

I split the cash in my hand, handing half to Nicky, then moved away from the atm towards the line of people waiting for bus tickets.

"I can't believe that worked." I breathed, wrapping my arm around Nicky's.

He bent down and kissed the top of my head, his eyes shuffling around the room as they always did. I studied the screens above the counter, feeling a sense of growing anxiety like Nicky did. We'd pulled the trigger and had to find a bus leaving as soon as possible. We didn't have much time to wait. Maybe not even thirty minutes. It was nearing three o'clock now, and while there was in fact a bus leaving at exactly three, the line was moving slow, and we had to get tickets onto that bus, wherever it was headed.

It felt like hours that we waited, watching the clock, the minutes ticking down. Of course, we only had to wait in the line for five minutes, but when you're in a position where every second counts, even moments feel like centuries.

"What can I do for you?" the man at the counter asked us.

"Two for the three o'clock." I mumbled, crumpling the cash a little in my hand.

"You're in luck. We have only six seats left. Lots of people are eager to get out of town today."

"Why is that?" Nicky wondered.

"It's Thanksgiving this weekend?"

"Oh, right, right."

My heart sank. It had been years since I'd properly celebrated Thanksgiving, but seeing everyone around us happy and excited about their plans made me realize just how ostracized we'd made ourselves. Even if we wanted to, we couldn't have those experiences. It was disappointing. A true reminder of all that we'd done. All that I'd done.

"Well, have a great day and a good holiday!" the man finished, sending us away with a wave.

"You too!" we said in unison, throwing our hoods back up and rushing back out into the cold.

Our timing was perfect. The bus was waiting for us as we pushed ourselves through the doors to our steaming metal ride. This bus in particular made deafeningly loud hissing noises as it regulated its insides, not entirely making itself welcoming.

None of that mattered, though.

A group of middle-aged ladies stepped up before us, then another young guy stepped on behind us, so we were limited in the remaining places to sit. The only seats open were near the emergency door on the side, dead center of the bus. The seats there were crammed and few, explaining why the women in front of us didn't choose them. We were less picky, though, throwing our stuff down at our feet and settling in.

I grabbed onto Nicky's arm, laying against him, truly just wanting to curl up in his lap. He held my good hand, resting his head against mine. This was starting to become familiar. Him and I. Close and comfortable. I realized I was getting used to it. That thought scared me a little. I didn't know what losing him would do to me. I almost found myself believing that I couldn't lose him; it would almost certainly kill me.

But, maybe it was better to love and lose than to never love at all.

Chapter 14

"Want one?" Nicky asked, offering me some Goldfish out of the bag he'd opened.

I took one, resting it on my tongue so it would soften. My stomach was annoyed with me, but I knew if I suddenly bombarded it with food, it would hate me even more. I could tell Nicky watched me from the side, waiting for me to swallow it. I took his hand in mine, petting the top of it with my fingers to let him know it was alright. The feeling of my skin seemed to settle him, and I felt him relax deeper into his seat.

The sun in the distance was beginning to set, its violent rays glowing with softer oranges and reds and pinks. It filled my eyes with more sustenance than could satisfy my stomach. It provided a calm and certainty of what was to come. As the last fizzling lights of the sun disappeared behind the clouds, out of sight from where we were, a gentle purple darkness would replace it. That darkness had such a strong power. With its presence alone, it would send a hush across the world, sending it to sleep to recover and recuperate. It was demanding in that way, not intending to scare or harm, but be a guide to health.

What the sunset and forthcoming night could not control, however, were the people. The animals may quiet, the tides may shift, but the people will forever continue to live as if daylight exists eternally. I don't think that the idea of that is necessarily bad, but, when it comes to the cost of one's health? I think my decision to get sober really opened my eyes to how unhealthy my choices were.

Working double shifts into the small hours of the night? Exhausting myself for no other reason than to exhaust myself. I didn't necessarily need the extra money. I just hated the idea of stopping. Of letting myself settle and quit moving, quit working, quit fighting to stay alive. I feared that if I stopped, I would drink myself to death.

Maybe that proves that I did care about my life a little. The fact that I held that fear of death. That I put myself in that position to limit my drinking. Even though it didn't work. Now, I wished desperately to go back and change it all, but that was impossible. I could only try to move forward. Let myself be influenced by the positive things around me. The changing of the days, the hope written in my soul, the words of those trying to help me. Nicky especially.

It was hard, but I could do that at least.

I took another cracker out of Nicky's bag and put it in my mouth. He smiled at me, clearly pleased to see me eating. I rolled my eyes, but was secretly glad he was proud. It mattered to me that he saw that I was trying. It was a motivation and reminder to take baby steps towards positive and healthy self-reliance. Not alcohol reliance or Nicky reliance.

I let my head fall onto his shoulder, rocking a bit from a turn the bus made. Someone's water bottle from a seat ahead of us fell into the aisle way as the bus finished the turn, banging harshly as the metal of the bottle hit the metal of the floor. The sound was piercing in my ears, echoing throughout the interior of the bus as the bottle continued to ricochet. A few people groaned their complaints, but the worst of what the disturbance caused was the waking of a sleeping baby.

The mother and her toddler were just a few rows back and across from us, so I could see them when I peered into the aisle. She had moved the child over onto her lap, bouncing him on her leg to calm him. It did little to help, though. The boy kept screaming and screaming, shouting for something he didn't yet have the words for.

"Can she shut that kid up?" a guy in front of us muttered, grasping his seat as the bus swerved onto the highway.

The feeling of the bus speeding up underneath us was vicious, the engine moaning with the acceleration. I grabbed tighter onto Nicky's arm, tightening my hood around my ears. The chaos all around us was overwhelming, and the effects of my hangover were still working their way out of my body. I tried breathing deeply, focusing on Nicky's realness beside me, beginning to dread the coming weeks of withdrawals.

And, as if I'd wished it, there was silence.

Everything in the bus went dead silent for a moment. The people stopped their protesting, the baby quieted, the bus' fight of the speed ended, but only for a moment. I thought that it would last. Only, the silence gave me just time enough to look out the window and see the out of control vehicle barreling straight towards us.

I could see it so vividly as if everything around me was in slow motion. It was a red truck, almost the same color red as the hoodie the man wore who had assaulted us in the Shell. I could see every detail; the scratch marks on the front, the slight dent to the left headlight, the headlights themselves emitting a yellow glow that shone and reflected off the side of the bus. I could even slightly make out the look of the driver, hands clutched forcefully to the wheel, out of focus for a second, then locked dead on us. And not just "us" as in the bus, but us as in Nicky and I. It was heading straight for the emergency door we sat beside.

All I could manage was a brief gasp before impact was made. The sound was deafening. A loud crunching and ripping of different materials met my ears. I could pick out what I thought was glass, metal, and the fabric of the seats, but what else was there? Flesh? Bone? Nicky was flung out of his seat into the air as I was pushed to the ground on my back, falling on top of my backpack. The emergency door folded in on itself, forcing me out into the aisle as the seat was destroyed. Nicky landed as I stopped moving, his head bashing into the bottom corner of a seat farther down from me.

I tried to blink, but my eyes were frozen open, staring right at Nicky as he was showered in debris. My eyelids could only manage a tremble while my mouth and lungs regained their strength after the shock.

"NICKY!"

The baby from earlier picked up its screams again, other people yelling out unintelligible shouts. None as loud as mine, though. I knew that. I could barely hear anything else besides them. I sobbed uncontrollably, trying to force my legs out from under the crumpled door. I didn't know if I was hurt. All I could think of was Nicky, lying there with his eyes closed.

"WHAT THE FUCK!" a man's voice hollered, running down the aisle to where I was, tripping over my outstretched arm and almost stomping onto Nicky's face.

He was hysterical, fighting his way to the front of the bus.

"Watch out!" I yelled back, reaching out for anything to take hold of.

Eventually, I was able to connect with the seat across from me, taking hold of one of the metal legs with both my hands. Without any preparation or caution, I pulled with all my might, ripping myself out from under the door. It was difficult, but I managed to free my legs, scrambling up to my knees once I could move them again.

"Nicky! Nicky!!!" I panted, crawling my way to him.

I rolled him over onto his back, looking him over for any sign of life. His whole body was limp. I leaned over his face, clutching his head in my hands. As I held him, I felt it. Blood seeping out from the back of his head, spilling out from my hand that cupped him onto the floor.

"Oh fuck! Nicky? Nicky, can you hear me?" I cried, brushing my thumbs against his face.

He didn't move a muscle.

I drew his head up to my chest, cradling it against my neck. I could feel warm breath against my skin, slow and uneven breath, but breath all the same. I looked around me to see if I could find anything to stop the bleeding, my eyes darting as fast as my heart was beating. A beige shawl was laying on the ground beside one of the seats just out of the way of the glass. I reached for it, stretching my arm as far as it would let me without dropping Nicky with my other. I only just took it by the tips of my fingers, having to drag it against the floor before I could get a good grip. I immediately bunched it behind Nicky's head, holding it against the spot I thought the bleeding was coming from.

"Nicky? Please wake up, Nicky! Wake up. Wake up, Nicky. You have to wake up." I murmured to him under my breath, petting his eyelids.

I started to notice the commotion around me. People were screaming and howling questions and instructions. I looked up for a second to see if I could find anyone to lock eyes with for help, but no one paid us any attention. Everyone was rushing around, some climbing out windows or running behind us, kicking me in the side and back in their hurry. I pulled Nicky towards me, holding him to my body and hanging on for dear life. I didn't mind getting hurt if it meant protecting him.

Suddenly, I heard a sharp inhale of breath.

"Nicky?!"

Nicky leaned away, vomiting onto the floor beside us. His forehead licked with sweat and blood dropped towards the sickness as his abrupt realization of pain likely caused a fainting spell. I was quick to catch him, lifting his head back upright. His eyes lolled without focus as I tried to steady him, blowing air onto his face in an attempt to wake him. His lips leaked with puke, running down his chin onto my shirt. I waited a moment, unsure of what to do, then he seemed to suddenly wake up, gasping again as he had before, almost jolting out of his stupor.

"What happened?" he wheezed, his breath hoarse.

"The bus got hit and you smashed your head. I'm trying to stop the bleeding, but it's really coming."

"Are you okay?"

"Yes, I'm fine. I'm worried about you."

"Kas?"

"Yeah?"

"We have to get out of here."

"Yes, of course? What do you mean?"

"The police. The first responders will be coming. We can't be caught."

"Nicky, I'm fine with that. Let them get me, so we can get you to a hospital."

"No."

"Nicky, I'm serious. I want to do this."

"NO!"

I faced him fully. There was a dead serious look on his weak face. I didn't have the strength to disobey him.

"Let's sit you up, then." I said, doing my best to haul him up by his armpits.

I managed to get him resting against the seat he'd hit himself on, but I could feel just how little ability he had.

"Here, hold this to your head." I told him, giving him the shawl I'd been pressing into him.

He took it from me, then grumbled angrily. "We have to hurry!"

"Hold on! Damn it, Nicky!" I shouted back, trying to hoist him up as he lunged forward in an attempt to stand.

He was so much bigger than I was that I wasn't much help at all. I did my best, though, leaning him onto my shoulder and maneuvering him around towards the front of the bus.

"No, no, Kasi, we can't go that way!"

"What? We can't get out any other way."

"Yes, we can." His finger moved across our bodies towards where we'd been sitting minutes before.

I turned and saw the gaping hole in the side of the bus where the metal had folded and the glass had shattered. The red truck was pinned up against it, black smoke the color of soot rising out from under the hood. It was possible to slip out and down onto the ground, but it was dangerous and much too technical for someone who could barely stand.

"No, fucking way, Nicky."

He didn't respond, taking a clumsy step towards the seat and throwing one of his knees onto what was left of it.

"Backpack."

"What?" I sputtered, rushing up behind him

"Grab the backpack!"

I looked down to where I'd fallen onto it, finding it there covered in glass and blood. As I bent down to grab it, I realized the blood was my own. My pants had been ripped when I was pinned under the door and blood was leaking out from my scraped shins. My hand has begun to bleed again as well; I could feel it pulsating underneath the bandage, beginning to soak through the gauze. There was nothing I could do about either of those things now, though, so I simply yanked the backpack up onto my shoulder, taking hold of Nicky under the other one.

"Go slow, please." I urged him, stepping up onto the debris, guiding him forward behind me.

He stumbled climbing up, dropping his hand that was holding the shawl to his head to steady himself. The shawl that had been cream tinted when I first saw it was deep wine colored now, soaked with blood. As Nicky squeezed it in his hand, blood dripped onto the emergency door, smearing along it like it'd been painted. My breathing went rampant at the sight of how badly hurt he was, my adrenaline pumping through my body like fiery, hot oil.

I don't know where I got it from, but from somewhere within myself I conjured the strength to grab Nicky around the middle, hauling him up onto my lap, and scooting us both underneath the cavity that had been the window. Once we'd passed through, it was a one foot drop onto the hood of the red truck, still smoking violently. We didn't have an opportunity to be careful about burning ourselves, so I didn't wait to check before throwing my feet down in front of me. My ankles tingled from the impact, but I steadied myself, reaching back up to help Nicky.

"Kasi, where are you?" he choked.

His eyes were closed, his hands both clutching the back of his head. I didn't know where the shawl had gone, but it was no use to us now. Nicky was starting to lose consciousness again. I had to get him down before that happened.

"Give me your hands. Your head will be alright for just a second." I plead, grabbing onto his jeans and pulling him towards the edge of the door.

With undeserved trust, he held out both his blood-covered hands, squinting his eyes down at me. I took one hand and one forearm, drawing him closer. As he reached the end of the emergency door, he fell forward onto the truck hood, landing straight into my arms. It was a miracle I held him up, but I did. We both stumbled a little, but I was able to keep us upright, eventually lowering us down into a crouch so it would be easier to slide off.

"I'm gonna go first, okay?"

Nicky nodded, disoriented.

I dropped to my butt, slipping off over the side of the red truck onto the ground. I instructed Nicky to do the same, catching him once again despite the excruciating pain I was beginning to feel in my hand. I wasted no time wincing with it, though, immediately throwing my arms around Nicky and walking us around the truck. We had to stumble through the tall grass in between the differing highway lanes to get to the other side, but we coped with it quickly, returning to the concrete near the back of the bus.

"Nicky, there's nowhere to go except the woods."

Nicky coughed, trying to catch raspy breaths. "Let's go there, then."

I strained myself against the weight of him, moving us forward past the bus, across the berm, and into the ditch on the other side.

There was a wired fence lining the treeline, but I could see a small break in it from a fallen limb. I headed directly for it, heaving Nicky up and over the branch and into the trees beyond.

It was pitch black dark once we left the safety of car headlights and the last remaining bits of sunlight. I could only see a little ways ahead of us, feeling only the crunching of leaves and sticks beneath my feet. I had no idea where to go or what to do. I only knew that I had to keep going. I had to get Nicky somewhere safe so I could help him. He would bleed out and die if I didn't soon.

The thought of that gave me strength. It also gave me tears, but I couldn't see anyway so it didn't matter that they filled my eyes. I tried controlling the sobbing as we walked, saving myself for whatever it was I would have to face next. All that kept me grounded was the feeling of Nicky in my arms, weak but present.

I don't know how long we walked, but it couldn't have been more than ten minutes. We were far enough away from the roadway that we couldn't hear the sound of cars or, more importantly, sirens, but I knew we could make it back to the highway if we needed to.

There was no good place to stop and treat Nicky's wounds because the woods were so dense; trees lined almost shoulder to shoulder, the rest of the open space taken up by briars and naked bushes. I'd just resolved myself to make do with the next good stump I saw when Nicky's arm suddenly flung into the air, pointing at something.

"Kasi, what's that?"

My eyes followed his finger towards a large dark shape in the distance. At first, I didn't know what to make of it, but then I noticed the outline of a door facing us, and I realized it was some sort of hunting hut.

"Holy shit."

Chapter 15

I practically sprinted for it, dragging Nicky behind me, rushing towards the hope of somewhere warm and enclosed. When we reached it, it was obvious it had been abandoned for some time, the wooden outside rotting away in large chunks. Although I should've been, I wasn't disheartened, trying the doorknob with an unnatural amount of faith.

It didn't open.

"Okay, um, Nicky, lean against here for a second." I said, flustered, helping him up against the side of the building.

He didn't argue, having become scarily quiet within the past few minutes. His deterioration terrified me, making me panic a bit in my desperation. I shook myself as I analyzed the door, trying to figure out how to open it. I looked around for a long, sturdy stick or branch, but my eyes were too filled with tears to see much of anything. I had only one option.

I positioned myself with my right shoulder facing the door, holding my hands against my stomach. With a cruel grunt, I threw myself against the door, slamming my body into it with the final fragments of my adrenaline. It didn't fly open like I'd imagined it, but the wood began to crack, breaking a bit down the seams. I tried it again, thrusting into it, crying out from the impact. The second time I made much more progress, the cracking sound louder in my ears. I knew it would only take one more good hit before it broke off.

"FUCK!" I shouted, shoving my shoulder into the door with everything I had left.

The weak part of the rottenness snapped as I hit it, the boards falling backwards into the hut. I used my foot to kick away the splintered wood pieces around the door until it swung away from me, the lock having broken away from the rest of it. A wave of damp air collided with me as the door opened wider and wider, greeting me with an unpleasantness I wasn't excited for. We had no other choice regardless of how much I cringed from the smell.

I took Nicky back in my arms, shuffling him through the doorway and into the single room.

To my surprise, the inside had a lot more than I would've thought. It was truly just a fancy shed with room for cleaning a kill or hanging a gun, but whoever had owned this in the past had set up a couch across from the gutting table. It sat against the back wall covered in dust and mouse droppings, but it was better than the cold floor.

I hobbled over to it, holding Nicky with one arm while I threw my backpack down and took off my coat with the other. I draped my jacket down across a cushion, then set Nicky onto it, getting a good look at his face for the first time since we'd left the bus.

His eyes were glossed over and his lips trembled. He had blood dripping down the back of his neck and around onto his collar bones. His skin gleamed with extra sweat, his breathing unsteady and rugged. There were small shards of glass in his fluffy hair and the damage of others in the form of tiny cuts over his cheeks.

"I need to look at your head. Can you lean forward for me?" I asked him, shrinking into myself as the words left my mouth.

The truth was I was scared shitless. Nicky knew how to take care of these things. Not me. I didn't know what to look for or how to treat it. And, apart from all that, I was afraid of what it would look like and how I would react. I didn't want my emotions to get the better of me and keep me from helping him in this crucial moment. I could imagine myself seeing it and feeling such an emptiness of hopelessness, bawling to myself so hard that I couldn't breathe let alone help. I didn't want to fall into that. I didn't want to fall into that sober.

Nicky braced against the couch, using what little energy he had to move towards me. I crouched down a bit, laying his forehead against my chest while I slid my hands around his neck. His hair was wet and sticky with blood still protruding from wherever the wound was. It was such a mess I had to search extensively for it, parting his hair with my fingernails. I realized as I struggled to find it that I was beginning to fall apart; my hands had begun to shake. And beyond my hands, my chest.

"Kasi, breathe." Nicky mumbled into my neck, reaching his hands out to grab my legs.

I nodded, not knowing if he could feel it. "I'm sorry, Nicky."

He didn't respond, his hands falling limp. I was losing him. I had to do something and standing here looking for something I couldn't find wasn't working.

"Lean back again." I whispered, helping him straighten away from me.

I wasn't sure if he could manage sitting up, but I didn't have time to do anything about it. Instead, my hands dove to the backpack I'd thrown on the floor, pulling out the pharmacy bag with all our leftover wound care things. I didn't know what the best course of action was, so I just worked with what I knew. I knew that I needed to wash his hair off so I could see the bleeding source. I could do that with a soft piece of gauze and some water from one of the bottles we'd picked up.

I took both out, pouring a small bit of water onto the gauze, then standing up so I could hold Nicky to me once more. Being as gentle as I possibly could, I wiped the wet gauze across the back of his head, soaking up a bit of the gushing blood. I didn't necessarily "clean" it like I'd hoped I would, but smearing the blood aside allowed me to see exactly where it was flowing from.

I folded the gauze in half and pressed it against the spot where I pictured the wound to be, drawing away more and more blood. In a brief moment when the blood wasn't leaking like a faucet, I was able to part his hair and see straight to his scalp. What I saw was both as bad as I feared and not what I expected. He must've hit the sharp corner of the seat leg because the cut into his head was a clean slice rather than a bash or scrape. Although thin and relatively unsoiled considering, it was deep and long. He really needed stitches, but we didn't have that luxury.

Feeling more confident in myself and my understanding of what I was working with, I moved Nicky's head into the crook of my right arm so I could bend down and grab more dry gauze out of the shopping bag. His head rolled into my elbow like it was a ragdoll, bloodying my skin as well as his. The more time I wasted fiddling, the more consciousness he was losing.

Advancing as fast as I could without being rough, I placed the dry piece of gauze, half folded, onto the cut, pressing it down against his scalp. Then, I grabbed another one, unfolded this time, and laid it on top of the first piece for extra protection. I knew the next part would be difficult, so I propped him up against my chest once more, giving myself a full view of his head. This action freed both my hands, and with both my hands, I began wrapping the bandage around him. I made sure I went in a perpendicular direction to the cut, hoping I could squeeze both sides of his flesh together as an acting stitch.

It wasn't pretty and it wasn't perfect, but when I finished, there was no more blood dripping down the back of his neck. I took that as a good sign.

"I'm done, Nicky, can you lay back?"

"How bad is it?"

I hesitated. I truly didn't know. "You're gonna be fine. The bleeding has stemmed a little. That should help. Just rest, now, okay?"

"Um, Kas?"

"Yes?"

One of Nicky's hands reached into his coat and pulled something out. I didn't care to see what it was, looking only into his eyes.

"If I die, could you give this to my sister?"

The letter in his hand was red-stained and crumpled, but he pushed into me, releasing it and letting it fall down into his lap. At the sight of it, I crumbled, loud sobs escaping me.

"Please?"

I covered my mouth, quaking with the effort of remaining still and not throwing up. "No. You're going to give it to her, Nicky. You have to."

"But, if I can't?" he wheezed.

"If you can't, I will, but that's not going to happen okay?"

"Okay."

I moaned against my hand, tears streaming down my face. I felt so crushed by the weight of it all. This wasn't fair. Not to Nicky. I hated it. It filled me with such immeasurable, sorrowful rage. I wanted to scream. I wanted to fight. I wanted to tear this building apart rotten piece by rotten piece, destroying myself in the process. I wanted everything to go away. I wanted to disintegrate. I wanted Nicky to survive. I wanted him to be able to get his letter to his sister. I wanted that more than anything in the world.

"Keep your eyes open and try to stay awake. I think it's probably good to keep you conscious for a while." I sniffled.

I could tell he struggled with that. His eyes were foggy and his blinking slow. To comfort me, however, he gave a weak thumbs up, saying something that I couldn't hear. I smiled back at him, not fully believing that I had just done everything I had.

The fleeting moment of relief at having accomplished one major goal passed quickly. I didn't know much about first aid, but I remembered how important it was to keep someone warm if they've had a lot of bleeding. This hut wasn't very well insulated, and with the sun having completely set now, it was only going to get colder. We had no other coats than the ones on our backs and under Nicky, so I had to find something else to wrap him up with. I didn't care if I froze.

There wasn't much around the hut in terms of storage, but there were a few lockers beside the gutting table. I opened one of them, unsure if someone might have left a backup coat here, but I found nothing inside except a few arrows and a picture of a five point buck. I was less hopeful going through the second one, and my hopelessness was met with the same disappointment. The second locker was completely empty apart from some mouse poop.

"Fuck." I whispered under my breath, looking around me for any other place where someone might store things.

My eyes locked on an old leather bag nestled up against the opposite side of the couch to Nicky. I think I'd marked it off as being full of hunting equipment when I first scanned the room, but now I had to check. It was dust covered and locked at the top with a small metal clasp that I had to fight with to loosen. When I did, though, I was shocked to find it full of slightly moth-eaten fleece blankets.

"Yes!" I cried, practically ripping the bag apart to pull them out.

The clasp had prevented any mice from getting in and the moths hadn't gotten to it too badly. They were pretty alright to say the least and would definitely keep Nicky warm. I took a couple in my arms, wiping off the rest of the couch and spreading them out on the other cushion, covering what I could of the old musty surface.

I helped Nicky stand for a moment so I could put another under where he had been sitting. When I set him down again, he instantly laid down, not bothering to move his feet from the floor. To supplement the effort he didn't have, I lifted his legs up onto the other side of the couch, finishing by draping a final blanket over him and placing my folded jacket behind his head as a pillow.

"Are you staying awake?" I asked him, wiping away some of the blood on his neck with my hand.

"Mhm." he replied, sleepily.

"Can I get you to drink something?"

He groaned.

"I know, I know. Can you, please?"

He scrunched up his face in disgust, but nodded nonetheless.

I opened up a new water bottle, giving it to him to take a few sips. I then drew some more crackers out of my backpack, convincing him to take just a few. I could tell how hard he was trying to stay awake, shaking himself occasionally when he drifted. Even so, he didn't complain, doing everything I asked of him while I simply knelt beside the couch, offering him food and water and petting his head.

The more time went on, the more my heart rate dropped, and I began to feel everything settle within me. As my adrenaline went down, the physical toll the crash had taken began to feel more real. My shins had stopped bleeding, but they ached whenever I moved, the raw skin burning against my pant legs after I'd changed into a new pair. I found myself picking out pieces of glass from my hair as well as bits of sticks and leaves from our trek through the woods, too. Compared to Nicky's injury, however, this was minor.

I could handle those things. What had started to worry me now was not an injury I sustained from the accident, but an injury I'd been sporting for a while. All the intense lifting and pulling had butchered the bandage on my hand, tearing open parts of my skin that I could feel had scabbed. I couldn't quite tell if the bleeding was as bad as it had been before, but, to the touch, the outside of the bandage was warm and damp.

I'd used the last of the gauze and bandages on Nicky's head, so there was no replacing the fragments of material wrapped around my hand. I didn't dare ask him what to do, yet, even though it was really starting to scare me. My solution was to ignore it. Don't look at it. Don't touch it. Don't think about it. I could only think about getting through the night. We could make a plan tomorrow.

"Kasi?" Nicky unexpectedly mumbled, reaching out to take my good hand that I'd rested next to him.

I hadn't realized it, but I'd been drifting in and out of sleep as I hovered beside the couch, watching Nicky to make sure he didn't die. I didn't know how long I'd been asleep, but I did know the room had gotten colder and even darker if that was possible.

"Are you okay? Is there something wrong with the bandage?" I asked, sitting up onto my knees.

Nicky laughed a little. "Yes, yes, everything's fine. I'm feeling better. Thanks to you."

"Really? You're not fucking with me?"

"Yes. Honest. Everything you did helped. I can see straighter, the room is not as blurry, and I can think more clearly. It hurts like hell, but I can feel the bleeding stopped."

"Good. Oh, I'm so glad. That scared me so bad, Nicky. I don't know. I thought you were gonna-"

"I didn't. I'm not, Kasi. You saved me. Thank you."

"You would've done the same thing for me."

Nicky bit the inside of his cheek, sighing heavily through his nose. I knew he was hurting.

"Are you warm enough?" I asked him.

"Yeah, but I could be warmer."

"Do you want me to look for more blankets? I only found these, but maybe there are more. Or I could lay my jacket over you-"

"Kasi, I just want you."

I watched as he lifted the blanket up, scooting away from the edge of the couch to make more room. I hesitated, then crawled onto the cushion, curling myself up against him. He tucked the blanket back over us, keeping his arm wrapped across my stomach. I could feel his nose brush up against my ear, then I felt his lips press gently into my neck. He only pecked me once, relaxing his head in my hair afterwards.

"Can I sleep now?" he asked me, whispering drowsily.

I rolled myself around to face him, sliding my arm up his back, scratching him carefully. He seemed to like it, groaning softly in his throat as he closed his eyes.

"I think you can. If I fall asleep, wake me up if you need anything, okay?" I told him, massaging his back with a lighter and lighter touch.

It was as if my fingers were a lullaby, singing him to sleep with every touch. I could see the moment he finally fell, his face unclenching, his breathing slowing. He was so peaceful he could've been dead. But, he wasn't. I could feel his chest expanding and contracting against my own, working almost in time with my lullaby.

I woke with a start. I seemed to have rolled over again in my sleep, so all I could see was the gutting table across the room from us. It was either very early in the morning or still very late at night. The sun had yet to peak out from behind the clouds, so darkness surrounded me. Nicky's arm was still strewn across my chest, his hand holding onto me softly. The room still stunk of the mustiness of abandonment, but since I'd fallen asleep, it had grown to smell strongly of metallic blood. I could practically taste it on my tongue, the smell was so pungent.

I took Nicky's hand in my fingers, brushing the back of his knuckles gently.

It was cold. Frozen even.

I sat up wildly, whipping around to face him. I realized as I moved, my hair was sopping wet, sticking to the back of my neck as if it had been glued there. The back of my shirt was soaked too, clinging to my skin with its cold moisture. And, there was that smell again. The rotten smell of blood. I placed a hand behind me to push myself the rest of the way around, but as my hand met the blanket covered cushion, it practically splashed with the liquid that drenched the back of me.

"Nicky?!" I gasped, grabbing his face with both hands.

His entire face was blood-covered from his forehead to his lips to his chin, then all the way down his neck and onto his chest. Both ears were dripping, his hair the worst of all. The bandage I'd wrapped around his head was no longer the tan color it'd been before, but instead a deep, sucking red.

I spread the blood around with my thumbs, trying desperately to process what I was seeing. All the blood I could feel was cold. Just about as icy as the room around us. He had bled long ago.

"Nicky? Wake up, Nicky!" I panted, my body beginning to shiver from the core.

He didn't stir.

I laid my head against his chest, listening for a heart beat.

Silence.

"NICKY?" I gasped, moving to my knees.

I took his shoulders in my hands and shook him. I shook him again. And again. And again.

"Nicky, don't fucking do this to me! Nicky, wake up!" I shouted at him.

I threw the blankets off of us, dragging him to a sitting position. He immediately fell backwards to where he'd been laying before. I screamed, shaking him again. He didn't move.

"NICKY!"

I jumped up onto my feet, reaching my hands up to my head. I dug my fingers into my scalp, pulling hair away from it, biting my tongue as hard as I could to keep myself quiet. I turned away from him for a second, then revolved back around, tears running down from my eyes like rain. My knees buckled beside him, my body falling forward towards him. I clung onto his lifeless form, sobbing into his blood-soaked hair.

"Nicky, come back! This can't be real!" I cried, drooling a bit onto his cheek.

I'd failed. I'd killed him.

The shivering in my body erupted into near convulsions. I was starting to hyperventilate, feeling every bit of myself disappearing like I was being erased. My head began to cloud, my vision darkening so I could hardly see a thing. I could only feel Nicky's frozen body and all the cool blood.

I tried to stand up again, fearful of how intensely my mind was leaving me. I backed up, moving my feet quickly and unsteadily. Without looking where I was going, I shuffled away farther and farther, keeping my eyes pointed in Nicky's direction. My arms twisted themselves around me in a hug, clutching onto my physical form to keep my mind from escaping. It seemed to want to go with him. To leave my body void of soul.

Suddenly and almost poetically, my feet caught on one of the straps of my backpack. I tripped heavily, throwing myself backwards in the process. As my upper body began plummeting towards the floor, my head got caught on the corner of the gutting table. I could hear my skull crack against it, splitting open my flesh like the seat leg had done to Nicky's.

I couldn't scream. I felt the scream burning inside me, but I couldn't release it. It rapped on the inside of my lips, pounding against them, begging to be let go. But, I couldn't.

I slid down the side of the table until my butt and legs were flat against the floor. I could see Nicky still draped across the couch, his arm strewn out as if he were waiting for me to lay next to him. It was almost too easy to envision myself there. It seemed as if that was exactly where I belonged.

But, I wasn't there.

I reached a hand up to the back of my head, feeling around for where the table corner had hit it. The wound was large and profuse amounts of blood were emptying it, pooling on the floor below me. It never stopped gushing. It wouldn't stop gushing. Not until my heart stopped pounding.

I couldn't scream, but I managed a sob, blinking some vision back into my eyes so I could see Nicky. He looked so peaceful. He *was* so peaceful. In death he was as beautiful as he was in life. The only difference was he had no warmth. My favorite part about him. I had always associated myself with the opposite of warmth. Cold. Evil. But, he? He was everything warm. Everything good. And we were both going to die anyway. It wasn't fair. Why couldn't he live? He was good, wasn't he?

"Oh, Nicky," I whispered, closing my eyes, picturing him with a bright smile on his face. "You were everything."

Then, the blood stopped. And I woke up.

Chapter 16

My chest swelled in a violent gasp. When I opened my eyes, I was staring at the bright ceiling, seeing small bits of dust float around the room. From head to toe, I was drenched in sweat, leftover tears trickling down my cheeks. My whole left side was numb except for my hand that ached with rage. I moved my arm out from underneath the cover of blankets, looking to see the source of the pain. Streaks of red beneath my skin ran down from my wrist, flowing purposefully towards my heart.

"I'm alive. It was only a dream." I whispered, shakily, turning my palm away from me to find more lines streaked along my hand.

I wasn't a medical expert, but I knew what this was. Blood poisoning.

The work we'd done to prevent the infection in my hand from getting worse hadn't done anything. The warmth I'd felt before under the bandage was not blood, but pus, and it had already gone beyond that icky stage and was now slowly killing me. It explained the dream and the sweat as well as the unending throbbing. I was alive now, but I wouldn't be for long.

I closed my eyes again, watching the back of my eyelids replay with a grotesque vividness the events of what I'd dreamed. It felt so real at the time. The pain, the panic, and Nicky-

"Nicky?" I half-shouted, shooting up to face him.

His eyebrows scrunched together when I called his name, furrowing together to form a solid line. He then drew his arms up to stretch them above his head, squinting his eyes open to look at me. The second I saw them glowing, I reached forward to kiss him. His lips were so warm. So warm unlike they'd been in my horrid imagination. He was here and alive and somewhat well. I grabbed his face with my good hand, throwing my leg up onto his, practically tackling him.

"Kasi?" Nicky mumbled against lips. "Are you okay?"

"Yes, why? Are you?"

"I'm great, but you're burning. I think you have a fever."

I sat away, pressing a hand to my forehead. "Am I?"

"And you're soaked with sweat. Kasi, something's not right."

Nicky placed a hand on the side of my cheek, feeling my temperature for himself. My lips quivered with a sudden wave of a chill, and I shut my eyes tight.

"Kasi? You know what's wrong, don't you?"

I nodded. "I don't want you to be mad."

"Why would I be mad?"

"Because it's my hand. I knew it was getting worse, but I never told you the truth all the times you asked."

"Give it to me."

I drew it out from under the blankets, shoving it into his chest. I could sense him sitting up beside me and opened my eyes to watch.

"I'm sorry." I told him as he began to examine the obvious signs of my condition.

"You have nothing to apologize for. I know why you didn't tell me. I know you just wanted to protect me. But, Kasi, you can't. Not forever. This is proof."

"I just know how much you've done for me. It's not fair how much you've sacrificed. I had to choose you last night."

He looked up at me. "What do you mean by that?"

"I used the last of the gauze and bandages on your head."

"Kasi, no-"

"You would've done it for me. You can't deny that."

"Then we're both idiots."

I felt the abrupt urge to be sick. I quickly yanked my hand away from Nicky, lurching over the back of the couch. Most of what I brought up was bile, the acid burning my throat, but I noticed small bloody bits in there, too. I realized my symptoms could be just as much from alcohol withdrawal as they were from the infection. I'd fucked up my stomach for over half a dozen years by overconsuming the equivalent of gasoline. It was no wonder I brought up blood when I vomited.

Nicky was behind me instantly, pulling my hair back around my ears. I could feel it sticking to my wet skin that still procured active sweat droplets. As hot as I was, I had never been colder. The sweat felt like someone was pouring ice water down my back. Not even Nicky's touch could make me feel differently. The only thing that gave me any contrast of temperature was the singeing of stomach acid in my throat and nasal cavity, but neither of those things exactly comforted me.

"Kasi, I know you're hurting right now, but I have to take your bandage off."

"I know." I groaned, turning back around and regiving him my hand.

The bandage was already falling off anyway, so it took little effort for him to pull it off completely. Once he removed it and the gauze, we were both exposed to the horrors of what neglect of a wound can do.

The length of the cut was the same, but the width had increased, leaving only a wafting hole of decaying tissue covered in a grayish-yellow pus that oozed out of the wound dramatically. All around my hand, the skin was a deep red hue, extending to the lighter red of the streaks down my arm. Beyond looking vile, it smelled so putrid I immediately wanted to be sick again. The scent in my nose stuck like a fly to a fly trap, smelling of rotten flesh.

"Fuck, Nicky." I whined, shying away.

Nicky didn't say anything for a few minutes. I had a dark suspicion of what he was going to say when he did speak again, and I desperately hoped I was wrong.

"Kasi, we have to make a decision." he finally said, still holding my hand in the palms of his own.

"I know."

"We have to get you help. That is a must. But, if we do, we can't run anymore. We can't keep hiding. We're going to have to face what happened in that Shell. The idea of that is terrifying, but what is more terrifying to me is if we don't get you help. The infection is in your bloodstream, Kas. You're going to die if we don't do anything about this."

"I know."

"I think you know what my decision is, but I won't do anything unless you want me to."

"I know you won't."

I hated how true that was.

I hated even more how it had come to this. If I hadn't been so weak to fall into addiction, none of this would've happened. If I hadn't been so desperate for a drink, I wouldn't have cut my hand on that stupid knife.

Nicky's voice in the back of my mind rang out with disagreement. He wouldn't blame me for my addiction. He would understand. He *did* understand. He would tell me that it wasn't my fault. That the events that led to my poor life choices were against my control. He would have empathy for how I'd ruined my life and destroyed myself just to feel something. To feel like I got what I deserved. But, to him, I deserved so much more than to torture myself for something that wasn't my fault. And, I knew he was right.

Not until I met him did I understand what all of that meant. He was worth so much in my eyes. He was a priceless person albeit broken. If I could see him that way, if I could want him to have the world, then I could want that for myself, too. I had to see myself as worthy. I had to make the effort, regardless of how difficult it was, to do everything in my power to love myself unconditionally and nonjudgmentally. I had to. Nicky would.

Then, I had a twisted thought. After all those times I'd made up my mind to turn myself in for Nicky to be saved, I finally had an opportunity. By agreeing to this, I was guaranteeing my capture. I just had to communicate Nicky's innocence fast enough to whoever got to me first, then he'd be free. Free from prison. Free from the past. Free from me. I didn't want to let him go. The thought of it made me want to crumble and die. But, I loved Nicky more.

I could do both. I could take care of myself and take care of him. Then, after all this was over, we'd never see each other again, and he'd be safe. And, if I died before I could be saved, then Nicky wouldn't have to worry about me anymore. He'd be safe from me. It was everything I'd always wanted. Wasn't it?

"Okay." I sighed, bringing my hand to my chest and resting it across it.

"Okay?"

"I'll do it. We can get help."

Nicky narrowed his eyes, scanning my face with incredulousness. "You're serious?"

"Yes."

"Okay. Let's go."

"Your head?"

"Doesn't matter."

"Nicky-"

"I can get help, too, right? The faster we go, the sooner both of us are going to be okay again."

"You're right."

The next ten minutes were spent in a mad rush. Nicky stumbled around, gathering the mess I'd left on the floor last night and grabbing all our other personal belongings. He then took out every shirt we had left in my backpack and threw it on me, topping me off with my coat he'd used as a pillow the night before. I tried to help, but I was getting worse by the second. I had two more vomiting spells in those ten minutes, and afterwards, the nausea didn't lessen. We were running out of time.

When the ten minutes were up, we were out of there, both Nicky and I using the other as a crutch. Nicky had more strength than I did, but after all the bloodloss he'd had yesterday, traversing the dense woods to get back to any kind of civilization was treacherous. I had both arms locked around his waist, half carrying him half holding on. I had to be the guide since Nicky had been barely conscious when we'd walked through here before. The unfortunate part was everything looked so much different in the daytime. I knew the general direction we'd come from, but following the same exact path was impossible.

Despite all the obstacles, though, we made it. Before either of us knew it, we could hear the sound of cars speeding past on the highway, the brush getting less and less thick. I felt as if I could even smell the exhaust of the cars, a scent I never thought would be welcoming.

When we reached the wire fence at the edge of the woods, I realized we were nowhere near where we'd entered. There were no gaps to pass through where we were, so we'd have to climb over unless we wanted to walk for even longer. I didn't know how much strength either of us had left.

"Nicky, we have to climb."

"You go first, okay? I'll lift you."

"Wait." I stumbled forward onto my knees, throwing up more bloody stomach acid.

Nicky crouched down at my side, picking me up without letting me settle first. There was urgency in his movements. He knew as well as I how little time I had before becoming septic. As if I were a feather, he carried me to the fence, lifting me over it and setting me down on the other side. I fell again as he dropped me, but I scrambled up as fast as I could to help him get over, too.

"Give me your hand!" I shouted to him, reaching my good hand over to his.

He took it, pulling against me with a lot less force than I knew he needed to for me to truly be helpful. Like I did, Nicky fell once he got his other foot over the top part of the metal fence, ripping his pant leg in the process. I tried to catch him, but my whole body became limp as I made my way to him. I collapsed like a fallen tree, feeling not an ounce of power anywhere inside me. The only movement I made was the shaking. Every inch of me shivered with fever.

"No, Kas, please." Nicky sobbed, scooping me up and holding me to his chest.

It took him some effort to stand back up, but he managed, carrying me with him as he hobbled towards the road. I tried to speak, but nothing came out, my mouth only letting out small gasps of breath.

"HELP! SOMEBODY STOP! I NEED HELP!" he suddenly screamed, almost walking straight out onto the highway.

"Nicky! Careful!" I whispered.

"Kasi, I'm gonna set you down for just a second. It'll be just a second, alright. I promise."

"Mhm."

He put me down in the grass just outside of the berm. I wasn't able to sit up, but I kept my knees upright while I laid my head back into the cool ground. Out of the corner of my eye, I could see Nicky flailing his arms in the air, waving at the cars that passed. He was shouting, crying uncontrollably for anyone to stop. I was afraid he was going to get hit, but there was nothing I could do about it. I couldn't call for him. I couldn't grab him. I couldn't do anything.

Finally, when almost all hope had been lost, a small blue sudan slowed down, pulling over a few hundred yards ahead of us. Nicky bolted towards them, half-sprinting half-jogging with his hands still raised in the air. I couldn't hear the words they exchanged, but suddenly Nicky was back at my side, holding my face in his hands.

"Kasi? Can you hear me? They're calling an ambulance. It'll be here soon."

He sounded underwater, but I still understood. I nodded, my eyelids becoming too heavy to hold open. I felt Nicky sit down beside me, moving my head, so he could cradle it in his lap. I then heard another pair of feet join us, shuffling around in the gravel.

"You need anything right now?" a man's voice asked.

"Do you have any blankets or an extra coat or anything I could put over her?" Nicky responded.

"Sorry, son. I was just on my way to work. I only have what's on my back."

"That's okay. You need to stay warm, too."

"So, what's she got?"

I opened my eyes just a little to find the shadowy shape of a person standing over us. I only noticed a few details, glasses, a beard, slicked back hair, before I felt a wave of nausea and dizziness hit me. My head dropped in Nicky's lap, and I felt his hands cup my face, rubbing my cheeks gently. I was so cold, but Nicky's hands were like a sudden fire against my skin. I hadn't been able to feel that before.

"I think she's septic." Nicky mumbled, an obvious weariness to his voice that indicated tears followed.

"Where'd you guys even come from?"

"Do you know when the ambulance should be here?"

The man stuttered for a moment. "I think soon. They said they had a unit already on the highway that'll make a u-turn back this way."

At the same time the man finished his sentence, the wailing of sirens became discernable among the other traffic. The blaring grew louder and louder until it was right on top of us, accompanied by the sound of tires on the berm once it reached us.

There was so much commotion it was hard to really understand what was happening. I heard slamming doors, voices over a radio,

Nicky's voice explaining what had happened, then the sound of a stretcher being pulled out of the back of the ambulance.

Unexpectedly, gloved fingers pried open my eyelids, shining a bright light into them. I gasped, startled by the forcefulness of the EMT, but Nicky didn't move from my side, which offered much more peace than I could've ever asked for.

"Can you hear me, honey?" the female EMT, who held the flashlight, questioned me.

"My head is spinning." I weakly replied.

"We're gonna make it go away, okay? We just gotta get you up into the ambulance."

Nicky suddenly took me in his arms, carrying me himself over and onto the stretcher. Two more EMTs then lifted the stretcher into the ambulance, strapping me down to it as they went. I panicked when Nicky's arms left me, and I immediately lifted my head to look for his figure amongst all the blurriness. One of the EMTs pressed my head back down flat while another drew my hand out from where I'd been clutching it to my chest and began pouring freezing liquid onto it.

I screamed out from the pain, straining myself against the restraints, trying to pull my knees up to my chest.

"Nicky! Nicky!" I shouted, panicking despite all the voices trying to settle me.

"I'm here. I'm right here." he called back, breathlessly.

It sounded like he was in the ambulance, but he was far away from me. Maybe at the other end of the stretcher, keeping out of the way of the EMTs. A whimper escaped my lips instead of a reply, the room growing darker and darker even with my eyes open. I wanted to be with him. I needed to feel him beside me. But, I couldn't see him. I didn't know where he was.

The doors of the ambulance shut with a bang and the blasting of the sirens picked back up again. Everyone that was in the back rocked from side to side as the ambulance began to move, nearly spinning out as it floored it against the gravel. I could feel the speed increase the more time went on, the driver pushing it and pushing it, and I understood that to mean how desperate the situation was.

"Nicky?"

"Kasi, it's okay."

I felt a hand grab onto my ankle, rubbing my exposed skin. I wasn't positive it was his, but it was warm like his. I imagined it was him as I laid there, believing for the first time that I was actually going to die. We'd made it all this way and I was finally here, getting the help we'd sorely sought after, but I wasn't getting any better. I could feel myself going rapidly into shock. Although I was fighting it, I was losing consciousness. I couldn't see or really speak. It was difficult to breathe and all the muscles in my body ached. My hand was on fire; it felt as if my flesh was literally being burned off, sagging onto the floor like sopping bits of cake batter.

I was really going to die. After all of this. After everything we'd been through. I wasn't going to make it. We were too late.

There was so much happening all around me, but all of the sudden, I heard *his* voice. Despite it all, I could hear him so well. It was as if everything else in the world disappeared and all that remained were the two of us. His lips were so close to my right ear I could hear him breathing even though I couldn't see him. Warm gusts of air were blown onto my skin, practically healing me with whatever magic Nicky possessed.

I soon realized that it wasn't just air that was being blown into my ear, but rather words. And more than words, they were lyrics. It was a delicate, musical stream of a song I loved that held such a different meaning to me now than it ever had before.

Nicky was singing to me. He was singing *Creep* by Radiohead, his voice cutting out as he stifled real sobs in time with the lyrics in the first verse. As he regained his breath, he skipped to the outro, brushing his fingers along my forehead. He made it almost to the final line when his words got caught in his throat, his head falling against mine, his cries intense.

I finished it for him through whispers, feeling my own tears fall down my face as I was lost.

I was woken as we turned into the parking lot of the hospital. There were tubes sticking out of my left arm, and I'd been stripped of the many layers I'd been wearing down to just one. I wasn't quite able to open my eyes yet, but I could hear everything going on around me with much more precision. Nicky had picked up my right hand and was holding it with both of his, petting my skin in a repetitive motion.

"What are your names again?" the female EMT asked from somewhere behind my head.

Nicky sounded so exhausted. "Nicky Vargas and Kasi Walt."

The woman mumbled something into her radio that I thought sounded like "it's them".

The ambulance came to an unexpected halt and everyone in the back swayed on their feet and where they sat once more. The back doors opened the same second we stopped, and I managed to open my eyes to see five more people standing outside. I was surrounded as they pulled me out, wheeling me away from the ambulance and towards bright fluorescent lights. Nicky followed us, but just out of my line of sight. I tried shifting myself around the nurses and EMTs to catch a glimpse of him, but they seemed to be blocking my view on purpose.

"Nicky?" I yelled, attempting to sit up against the straps that held me down.

"Lay back." someone corrected me, putting a hand on my shoulder.

I fought against them, struggling with the little strength I'd regained. "Nicky?"

We turned a corner, stopping suddenly as a doctor walked out in front of us. The nurses fell into one another, clearing a small enough gap between them for me to see back out into the hall where the ambulance still was. Standing right by the door with his hands behind his back and two police officers cuffing him was Nicky.

I screamed out. "He's innocent! He didn't do anything wrong! It's all my fault! Don't arrest him!"

A nurse put a hand over my mouth to muffle my shouts, and as she did, I heard the worst words I could have possibly heard at that moment.

"Nicky Vargas, you are under arrest."

Epilogue

So, my plan didn't work after all. I wasn't able to save him from every horrible thing I'd envisioned.

I spent two weeks in the hospital recovering from my injuries. It was pure misery. My aggression towards treatment along with my brutal withdrawal symptoms meant most of my treatment consisted of being knocked out and woken up again and again until I acted reasonably. I was starving for answers about what had happened to Nicky. The nurses that had been with me the day I was admitted assured me he was fine. I knew they couldn't have known that. He wasn't white and he wasn't rich, and that immediately disintegrated any hope that assurance might've granted me.

I was asked several times if I wanted to contact my parents or a loved one. Everytime I told them I wanted to talk to Nicky. I begged them. I did everything I could to invoke a response. I refused meals and pain treatments. I made myself miserable to force them to pay attention to me. But, it didn't work. Nothing I did made them issue a word. Or even attempt to find the answers for me if they didn't already know.

Although, it was no secret I was here. Everyone knew. I could hear the nurses whispering about me in the halls and whenever I managed to get the tv on, I saw myself reflected there with the headline "they've been caught". Usually before I could tune in long enough to hear more information, the remote was taken from me. My rights as a patient were restricted because I had yet to be charged. I was a criminal. And, that scared people.

I could see it written so clearly on the faces of some of the nurses. They knew what I had done, and to them, I was capable of doing it again. There were assumptions and guesses as to what made me act in the murderous manner that I had, but no one but myself could answer the question as to whether I'd acted with malicious intent. I probably would've been afraid of me, too.

Apart from much mental suffrage, my body was in pieces. The sepsis was not too far gone when I'd been taken into care, but it was enough to damage me. I was admitted into the ICU at first, given a rapid dosage of antibiotics as well as intravenous fluids to keep my organs from failing. I was told by doctors that I was lucky to have survived. The daily wound dressings and invasive poking and prodding from the strangers around me made me not so sure.

What was even more intolerable, however, was the alcohol withdrawal. The hallucinations, panic attacks, the insane body aches, and above all, the unending craving for something to hurt worse than all of this. To just have one drink to suppress the other pain long enough for me to breathe. It was a gruesome challenge. One of the hardest things I've ever gone through. And without anyone there to support me, I was beginning to struggle with seeing the point of it all. But, every time I started to fall into that well of despair, I remembered Nicky. I couldn't allow myself to fail before I knew what had become of him. That small little prick of hope that he was okay and made it through and wasn't in prison, gave me the strength to keep going.

A public defender was notified when I was to be released from the hospital sometime near the eleventh day of my stay. He came to meet me on the morning of my release to give me information about my arraignment, but he also gave me information about Nicky.

He sat on a chair that had been pulled up next to my bed in the private room I'd been transferred to. It wasn't wonderful, but it was quieter than the ICU and I knew being relocated here meant I'd get to leave soon. That thought was a comfort to me. As for the defender, he was a tall and skinny man, maybe early 40s. He wore a rough-looking stubble and had great big bushy eyebrows, which alone were quite obnoxious and intimidating features. But, he didn't scare me. His eyes were gentle. Soft like Nicky's.

"My name's Theodore or Ted Bell, and I'm your public defender. Nice to meet you, Kasandra."

I pursed my lips and nodded. I still wasn't sure whether to trust him. No matter how soft his eyes.

"I'm so sorry to have to meet you like this. I hope your recovery is going well?"

I sighed. "I'm physically on the ups, but I don't imagine my health matters to you."

"It does to me at least. I'm here for legal reasons, but I'm still a human. I was devastated by your case."

"So am I."

"Of course. I'd just like to talk to you about what's going to happen moving forward. Legally. I'm not much help medically, I'm afraid."

I smiled without meaning to.

"Well, Kasandra, Nicky has already given a plea and been issued his charges. Because you were incapacitated, the judge allowed for some recovery time before pressing for your plea. If it is alright with you, I will read out your charges now as have already been discussed between the judge and myself."

"Are my charges the same as Nicky's?"

"I'm not allowed to give you that information."

"But, I was-"

I stopped myself, realizing what I was about to admit. I wanted so desperately to protect him even if it was too late. A very large part of me wanted to admit my intoxication on that night if it would pull guilt away from Nicky. But, another part of me was so afraid. Afraid of admitting something that could ruin my life.

The thing I had to realize, though, was that I already was. I knew that if I continued at the pace I was, I would be dead of alcohol poisoning within a few years. I knew I would be. If not now, I would ruin my life later. If I allowed myself to let things play out and let the law take control, maybe I could fulfill the promise I made to myself. And to Nicky. Maybe I could actually get sober.

I took a deep breath and looked straight into the gray eyes beneath the bushy brows. "That night. I wasn't sober. I have to be honest about that. Will it affect the charges?"

Ted kept a straight face, but his lip twitched. "No. In this state, intoxication can have an effect on self-defense laws, but in your case it wouldn't have mattered. Because there is video evidence of the crime, there is beyond a reasonable doubt that even if your ability to determine danger was impaired, your actions were a response to a threat."

"Wait-"

"Excuse me for one moment. Just let me give you the charges. It may help clear some things up for you."

He pulled out a paper from the briefcase he'd entered with and read aloud: "Kasandra Louise Walt, you are formally charged with a 1st degree misdemeanor of fleeing from the police and evading arrest. Given the nature of the misdemeanor and the circumstances in which the misdemeanor occurred, the penalties are decreased."

"But, I-"

"The law is aware of what you did, and they have ruled it as self defense. There is no audio on the security recording, but we believe you were verbally threatened before physically attacked. That alone is enough to justify what happened."

"Did Nicky-"

"I'm not allowed to discuss other cases," Ted glanced around nervously before bending low over the bed and whispering. "But, he has not been convicted of manslaughter. Or assault. He was more than a witness to the crime so he cannot be charged with failure to report. I'm not supposed to tell you this, but his charges aren't much different from yours."

I felt the knot in my chest untie, loosening around my ribs. For the first time in days, I could breathe without pain.

"Back to the point, however, I would like to ask you now if you have a plea in mind. If you are willing to give it now, it would make things go smoother. I can speak to the judge before your arraignment and your penalty, if you choose to plead guilty, can be arranged before your appearance. It would decrease its significance while also decreasing the time in which everything can happen. But, you are well within your rights to withhold a plea."

"For the misdemeanor?"

"Yes."

"Guilty. I plead guilty."

Another week later, I found myself standing in a courthouse bathroom, awaiting my arraignment. I ran my hands under the cold water until I could barely feel them, then placed both on my neck, feeling the instant burn of the temperature. Once my hands had warmed against my skin, I pulled them away, studying the new scar on my palm. I could see evidence of the stitches and the stark whiteness of my scar, but apart from the raised skin that remained, there was no evidence that it'd been oozing pus just a few weeks before. I still shuddered at the thought of it. It made me sick to see it, but I still liked to rub my fingers over it, thinking of Nicky.

When I saw my face in the mirror, I could hardly recognize it. My skin had cleared and my eyes weren't bloodshot. My dark roots had begun to grow out and the ends of my hair were damaged from all the bleach. But, it wasn't ugly. It was all a reminder of what had happened to me. What had happened to us. Nicky and I.

I missed him. I missed him so desperately. I hadn't been able to find him. Even after I was released from the hospital, my attempts at getting more information about his whereabouts or his health were fruitless. I looked up him, his sister, his address, anything that I knew was connected to him. But, nothing. It was almost as if he had never existed. But, I knew he had. When I saw myself in the mirror, I saw every trace of him. I could feel him so near to me.

There was a knock on the bathroom door. "Miss Walt, they're ready for you."

I opened the door to find Ted waiting for me in a straight-pressed suit, his face sagging with tiredness. I followed him out, pulling the collar of the shirt away from my neck. The courthouse was suffocating and I could barely breathe as it was. I could feel my pulse in every part of my body; from my ears to my throat to my fingertips to my ankles. Heat flooded me, but, as if I was a robot, I just kept walking. I moved myself forward, feeling everything and nothing at the same time.

"Are you alright?" Ted asked, looking back at me as we walked.

"Mhm."

"You nervous?"

"A little."

"Sure. Makes sense. Everything will work out as we discussed. It is very rare for a judge to change their decision in such a short amount of time."

I couldn't tell if that was supposed to make me feel better.

"Anyway, we're just in here." Ted pointed to a set of double doors with the number 114 just beside it.

Ted pushed down the handle closest to us open, striding inside with a confidence I couldn't match. The room we entered was small, and every second we remained in there, it kept on getting smaller. With carpeted floors and dark wooden walls, everything smelled stale, dust lingering in the corners of the space. Not a single wall held a window; the lack of natural light not helping to shake the feeling of a trap.

I was guided to a chair that stood behind a desk at the front of the room. Across from where I sat was a raised platform, just a single step up from the ground level. On it, perched directly in the middle, was another desk, but this desk had walls that sank all the way down, hiding whatever was behind it. A tall chair was mounted in its lap and sitting in it was an older woman with tightly thin lips and a black robe.

"Kasandra Louise Walt, you enter this courthouse today with the charge of police evasion. A 1st degree misdemeanor with a penalty of $800 and 2 years of probation. This came following an altercation that occurred in your place of work while you were on duty, which resulted in the death of one involved party. This court has already ruled that you acted out of self-defense, so you will not be charged with any form of manslaughter. Your plea was discussed previously between your public defender and myself, but I will ask you again in the formal environment of the court, how do you plea?"

Ted nudged me, indicating that I should stand. Before doing so, I took a deep breath, allowing it to fill me in entirety. It was not refreshing. It was not comforting. But, it was all I could do to keep myself from doubling over on the desk in front of me.

With shaking legs, I stood, locking eyes with the judge, but maintaining my cowardly stance. Even if I had the strength to stand straighter, I didn't have the heart.

"I plead guilty."

"Thank you. We will send you home with some information regarding your probation and the fines. I believe Mr. Bell has discussed what your probation will entail?"

"Yes."

"Then, I wish you luck, Miss Walt."

I nodded to her, unable to part my lips to thank her.

Moving just as robotically as I had before, I trailed Ted back out of the room and into the hall, then down towards the front room where a receptionist shared a few words with him. I was handed my coat back from the rack, then given a heavy yellow envelope.

"This is that information about your probation. It also has an envelope for you to send the fine in. You have my contact if you need anything further." Ted explained.

"Thanks. What do I do now?"

Ted sighed. "Go. You're free. Just don't do anything against your probation and you'll be free to live a normal life."

"Just like that?"

"Yes. Isn't that what you want?"

"Of course. It's just...after everything, this feels easy."

"You're lucky the law was in your favor and there was enough evidence to prove your innocence. You didn't get off easy if that's what you're thinking."

"I don't know what I'm thinking, really. I spent so much time thinking my life was over."

"It almost was. You nearly died. Multiple times."

"But, at the time, I almost believed that to be easier than having to face what I had done."

Ted took me by the arm and led me away from the counter and the people entering the courthouse. "What you did, Kasandra, was save your life. And Nicky's. I'm sorry that the incompetence of the justice system made you think any differently. I'm sorry it forced you to run, thinking it was your only option. And I'm even more sorry that you have to be punished for that."

"Why would you say that?"

"I just had a daughter, and not long after having her, I realized I'd do anything to protect her. I know how it feels to love someone so much that you're willing to throw everything away for them. When I took your case, I couldn't keep myself from imagining she was you."

"So, you pity me?"

"I see a world that I pity. I'm not working at a job that doesn't pay me enough because I enjoy it. I'm here because I figured one day I would meet someone like you who doesn't realize she deserves much more than what life's dealt her."

"How can you know that about me?"

"Because one of the very first questions you asked me was not about yourself. I'm not sure if you knew Mr. Vargas before this incident, but what you did showed me that you, someone who has little in this world, were willing to make the biggest sacrifice to prevent someone else from receiving that same fate."

"I don't know what to say."

"Say nothing. And leave. You deserve the freedom. You have somewhere to go, right?"

"I do."

Ted nodded back to me with tears in his eyes. I wasn't sure what to make of everything he'd just said, but I had no intention of staying another second in this suffocating building. With my coat over my arm, I made my way to the exit, taking less robotic steps each step towards the glass doors. Just as I laid my hand on the handle, I turned back to Ted, who had been watching me leave.

"Thank you." I mouthed.

Ted stood stoically with his hands in his pockets with the gentle look of a man who felt a great weight on his heart. I didn't know it at the time, but I'd never see him again. The memory of him and the words he said to me, however, would stay with me until the day I died.

The overcast day and crisp breeze welcomed me as I left the building, the sun setting behind the clouds. I watched my feet as I crept onto the sidewalk, finding the coolness a blast against the heat I'd felt inside. Everything about these past few weeks had almost felt like an illusion. I had felt as if I was on a conveyor belt just passing the days by without any real intention of going anywhere. Now, with each step

I took, I was beginning to feel realer and realer. I started to understand that it was all over. I'd made it to the point I'd been craving to reach. It was everything.

And yet, it wasn't.

I was missing something.

Halfway down the sidewalk that led towards the parking lot, I felt the sudden urge to look up. As I did, my breath caught and my eyes watered with what I was sure was another hallucination.

Standing there at the end of the sidewalk, staring at me with a soft smile on his face was Nicky. He hadn't changed a single bit. In all my imagination and all my hallucinations, he appeared in front of me just like that. He was a vision, glowing as if he was in a most wonderful dream. His hair curled around his face, blowing a bit in the wind, and his eyes held hints of the smile that rested on his lips.

I waited, holding completely still as I watched him, unsure if he was even there. A flood of everything we'd gone through together washed over me, and I felt as if I could faint. I could've drowned right there, gasping for breath from the weight of it all. But, despite myself, I took an unsteady step forward, inching my way towards him. He followed suit, taking one small step towards me, then another and another, each faster and faster until he was running in my direction.

He knocked into me, wrapping his arms around me and hoisting me up into the air. The instant we touched, I knew he was real. It was the warmth. I hadn't known that feeling since I'd last seen him in the flesh. During every nightmarish moment my brain had conjured him, he'd been frozen like death. I figured now I was either dead with him or it was real, and I had to believe it was real.

One of Nicky's hands reached up to the back of my head and held me as he set me back on my feet. I hadn't realized how much I'd missed his tenderness. I hadn't realized how much being free had meant nothing unless he was too. I knew that it was wrong to want him to really, truly be here now, but I couldn't help myself. I'd imagined this moment when everything was over, and I'd assumed I'd be happy that Nicky had gotten away from me. But, I wasn't. And here he was.

I looked up into his eyes and saw so much joy in them. They were watery with tears, but they were happy and alive. Just his eyes held so much more life than I felt in my entire body. At least, until this moment. Being with him unleashed a rage of an intense feeling within me. I wasn't sure what that feeling was, but it was nice to feel something other than the numbness.

Nicky took my face in his hands and brought his nose to mine. He nuzzled the end of it with his, his skin beginning to dampen from the tears on his face. As I felt his, my own welled up, pressing against my chest from the inside like a hand pressing down on a book. A body, a person other than what I was scrambled within me, bracing against my flesh to be released. Every tear I'd had yet to shed for my selfish feelings towards Nicky prayed on the downfall of my outward self. It wanted so desperately to be let go.

I could not let it.

"It's so good to see you." Nicky whispered, snot trickling down onto his upper lip.

I watched it, refusing to look back in his eyes. Now that I knew he was real, I was afraid to allow myself the privilege of his goodness. I couldn't look into him and see myself reflected there.

"Why are you here?" I asked.

"Why shouldn't I be?"

"Because, Nicky." I failed and caught his gaze. It was everything precious and innocent as I'd imagined it. I sucked in a sob as I went on.

"I ruined everything for you. You should be running away from me, not towards me."

"Kasi, what happened to us isn't something I can run away from. From the fucking moment I saw you disappear into that hospital, I knew that I wasn't content being without you. I'd shared things with you that no one else in the whole world would ever understand. For the first time in my whole life, I felt at peace in someone's presence. I've never had to hide in front of you. I don't think I'll find that again. Maybe it's wrong for me to be here now, but I don't care. I just needed you to know how I felt. I'll do whatever you want me to. If you want me to leave, say the word and I'll be gone."

I shook my head. "That's the problem, Nicky."

"What do you mean?"

"You're so good."

"Kasi-"

I pushed him away from me and took a few steps back. "You don't understand how much I care for you. I love you. I can't help loving you. What I feel for you is unlike anything I've ever experienced before. I'm cruel and I'm selfish, but you make me feel something. You make me feel like I'm a good person. But, I'm not that. I'm weak and I'm sick, and I never want you to have to take care of me again. I want to be able to take care of *you*. I want to be healthy so I can. But, I just don't think I'll ever be good enough or healthy enough to deserve you. You're everything. You have to stay away from me."

"Kasi, listen to me," Nicky's voice was stern. "In this messed up world, we're all just little people. You're just a person. You can't do everything on your own. Sometimes, you need and *deserve* to be taken care of. I want to be that for you. And, before you say another damn word, I know the reason you feel so much guilt about me being willing to offer that is because no one has ever taken care of or shown you that you are worth it before. You are such a wonder, Kasi. I will spend the rest of my life proving to you that you are if I have to. I don't want to be alone and neither do you. It's about sharing the burden, Kasi. I can't think of a single person on Earth I'd like to do that with more than you. Just accept that you are allowed to be loved."

"I'm so scared, Nicky. I don't want you to become another addiction. I don't want to be dependent on you to survive. It's not fair what I might subject you to. I don't know if I'm strong enough."

"When was the last time you had something to drink."

I went quiet, staring at him, thoughtfully. "Weeks ago."

"You overcame that without me. You made that choice for yourself. I promise you, you have the power to determine what our dynamic is to you. We'll work together to not make it an addiction, but a mutually beneficial coexistence. You are strong on your own. I only reminded you of how strong you really were. You're not strong because of me. I don't have to be another addiction. This can be healthy. I promise you,

"Kasi, I refuse to believe that we met by accident. I refuse to believe that I met you for no reason. I nearly died in that hut in the woods, and I know it sounds stupid to say, but it made me realize some things. I only have one life. Both of us do. We made it this far. Why not spend the rest together? Don't you want to?"

I gave him a look, biting the inside of my cheek hard enough to send a shock up the whole left side of my face. "I do, but it's selfish to want it."

"How come?"

"You deserve so much better than me."

"Kasi, I'm literally telling you that I want you. I'm telling you that I love you. You are everything that I will ever want and ever deserve just how you are."

"Truly?"

"Yes," Nicky's face grew into a smile as he came closer to me. He stood a foot away, holding out his hand for me. I took it. "We're going to have to work on you believing me. Let go of whatever voice in your head is telling you to push the truth away."

And then, all of the sudden, the girl inside me, who knew of the goodness within us, broke through the walls of her prison, rushing out to fill the gaps of me she hadn't been able to fill before. With full feeling in every inch of my body, I reached upwards to meet Nicky's lips. I kissed him slowly while allowing tears to fall and not suppressing the sobs. Nicky curled his arms around me, holding me close to his chest. The smell of him was like a sterilized wash, pouring over me and cleansing me of my self-hatred.

After a moment, I broke away because my sobs got too intense, but Nicky didn't stop. He reached down to kiss my neck, then my cheek, then my forehead, then my knuckles, then my palms. Between every kiss he'd whisper "I love you" quiet enough so no other soul could hear it but me.

I think I finally understood what it meant to be special. Not special because of anything I'd done. But, special because I was me. I was me and I didn't die. I survived and I was not alone.

And I never was again.

What it is to Bleed